DEEPER THAN DREAMS

A LOVE & STEEL NOVELLA

JESSICA TOPPER

lunabloom books

For all the dreamers.

~

"WHERE WOULD you find fairy tales on the library shelves, luv?"

Adrian's question sifted into my slumber, adding depth and dimension. I was vaguely aware of his warm skin against my cheek and his chest rising and falling in a deep rhythm.

"398.2," I recited, my voice drowsy from dreaming. "Why?"

"I love fairy tales," Abbey murmured to my left. Her small body stiffened in a long stretch before curling around my hip and leg, and her tiny hand pat-patted Adrian's where it was cupped around my shoulder.

"I'm just making sure you know where you're waking up."

Oh, I knew exactly where.

The three of us were all under one roof, in the twenty-six-hundred square feet of the Manhattan sky that was Adrian's apartment, waking up together for the first time. Some might call it a fairy tale, happily ever after and all that jazz. I was thinking more along the lines of the best kind of dream, finally come true.

I had, after all, dreamed of Adrian Graves before I had even met him.

"You're smiling, Kat," he whispered. "I can feel it."

My grin pressed against the spiral of his desert flower tattoo. Unlike the species it was based on, which took years to blossom and only opened for a few days at a time, Adrian's flower was always in bloom. It was more like the love that had inspired it: quickly growing, fresh, and beautiful.

"My favorite fairy tale of all is 'Goldilocks and the Three Bears,'" Abbey continued in her breathy, morning rasp. "My bed at home is too small. Natalie's bed down the hall is too big. But this bed? Just right!"

"Don't get too used to it," I warned her. "You've got school tomorrow."

Reality had been sucked into a surreal vacuum as I had watched Adrian perform last night as Digger Graves to a screaming, sold out crowd at his Madison Square Garden show. The concert had taken place on Halloween, which just so happened to have fallen on a Sunday.

"Mommy, do we have to go back home?" Abbey's small fist punched at the pillow in protest. "I don't want to go to school."

"Let's not think about tomorrow just yet." Adrian raked a hand through his wayward, dark blond hair. The only lingering evidence of last night's performance was a smudge of kohl liner under his right eye, reminiscent of Malcolm McDowell's creepy character in Kubrick's *A Clockwork Orange*.

My gentle menace kissed both of our foreheads in turn. "Let's think about . . . breakfast in bed. What shall we have? Beans on toast? Smoked eel pie?"

Abbey gave a delighted squeal of disgust, disturbing the kitten at her feet. She loved when Adrian waxed poetic on what she considered the humorous meals of his homeland.

"How about a full English breakfast for your mum?" he continued. "A proper fry-up that's old school, greasy, and gorgeous?"

Abbey giggled with every trilled *r* that rolled off his tongue. "What will Chelsea eat?" she asked.

The kitten was now up and stalking a loose thread from the sheet, pouncing as Adrian rolled out of bed and shrugged into a zip-up hooded sweatshirt. He was always careful to shield his "boogeyman" body art from Abbey's young eyes and imagination, lest she have nightmares about some of the more gruesome tattoos on display.

"Kippers for the wee little Chelsea?"

Whether my five year old even knew what a kipper was, I wasn't sure. But she clapped her hands and bounced off the bed after Adrian.

"A full English breakfast would be wonderful," I told them

both, propping myself up on my elbows. "Hold the black pudding, baked beans, and fried bread."

"So basically bacon and eggs?" Adrian laughed. "I can do that. But I need the help of a certain cat and trusty sidekick."

Ever a slave to PBS and her favorite TV show, Abbey pricked up her ears. "Maxwell MacGillikitty?" With zero hesitation, she added, "And Mr. Quackson, his dashing duck confidant?"

Although he had written the show's theme song in jest many years ago, Adrian respected Abbey's devotion to its cat crusader hero, and answered her in all seriousness.

"I'm afraid Max and the Mister are indisposed, Abbey. But you and Chelsea will do just fine." He gave me a wink, which threw my own imagination into overdrive. *Sexy man, entertaining your child*, as Marissa would say. My best friend had seen the potential in Adrian as soon as he strummed his first bar chord during that children's program he so graciously agreed to do at the library back in April.

Little had I known, I had pulled one of the world's most elusive hard rockers out of hiding and back amongst the living that day.

"Do they have spiral staircases in English?" I heard Abbey inquire, as they made their way downstairs.

"England's got loads of 'em! There are the Tulip Stairs at the Queen's house, for one."

"Have you ever been there?"

Adrian's laugh was faint to my ears, and his response was too far away to hear as they descended.

I smiled and stretched, reveling in the glorious view that was just beyond my fingertips. There was barely a need for curtains when you were set so high above Central Park, although I had no doubt some of the apartments on the East Side housed telescopes powerful enough to see right across to the West Side.

We had fallen asleep under the fattened Manhattan moon last night, and had awoken to a crisp, autumn day. The park was awash with golden browns, oranges, and yellows; its tree-tops like a seventies-era shag carpet I could imagine walking across. The foliage was still lush, although there were a few bare spots here and there where leaves had already found their way down to the ground. My smile turned into a sigh as I realized it was November first.

Some people reveled in flipping to a new page on the calendar, for them it was a time of new beginnings and fresh starts, and I didn't begrudge them that. Fate had just dictated a sadder habit for me, reminding me of loss with each passing of the milestone first of the month. So much, in fact, I couldn't bear to keep a calendar in the house until Abbey reached school age and necessity had warranted it. *Do we have to go back home?* Abbey's plaintive tone, entreating me, came to mind. *I don't want to go to school.*

School was in Lauder Lake, and Lauder Lake had been our home for the last four years. Sanctuary after our senseless loss. That September ist day had started like any other, and had ended in a memory I could never shake. I hadn't been able to stay in the city after Pete died. Home couldn't be where my husband had existed one day and not the next. So I had taken our baby daughter to the one place where I had existed before I knew him.

But I had just been living on autopilot there. Until Adrian stumbled—adorably and drunkenly—into our lives last spring.

And now here we were, back in Manhattan. I was happy, but sometimes found it hard to wrap my head around it.

"Over easy, luv?" Adrian bellowed.

"Scrambled, please!" I kicked down the covers, suddenly restless. I wasn't used to being waited on. "I can come down, please don't fuss."

"Don't come down yet!" Abbey screeched. "We're not fussing, we're busy."

I laughed to an empty room, shaking my head, and reached for some reading material. My fingertips fell on the red-leather binding of Blake's poetry. Adrian had read from the book the first time I had visited—not long after I had discovered the legendary identity of my new lover. The memory felt like an old one. He'd had a MetroCard marking his spot that day, conjuring up images in my mind of him entering the subway with both in hand and winding under Manhattan for hours, lost in Blake's world of words.

Today there was a new marker holding his place on a different page. Adrian had underlined select passages, and certain words were even circled with inky emphasis.

I seize the sphery harp, strike the strings!
At the first sound
the golden Sun arises from the deep,
And shakes his awful hair;
The Echo wakes the moon to unbind her silver locks:
Arise and drink your bliss!
I wake sweet joy in dens of sorrow,
and I plant a smile
In forests of affliction,
And wake the bubbling springs of life
in regions of dark death.

WITH A SMILE, I couldn't help but wonder if Adrian had been pondering the poetry, or dreaming up new song material inspired by such heavy stanzas. I loved Blake's imagery of golden suns and silvery moons. The actual sun chose to shine strong as I glanced back up, setting the trees ablaze in glorious light and warming my face.

Arise and drink your bliss!

Perhaps it was time for new beginnings.

I moved to stow Adrian's place marker, realizing it was an envelope as its unsealed flap caught on the pages. *Digger & Kat* was inked across the front in neat, narrow script.

I had only met Adrian's best friend and bandmate in person once, last night, but I recognized Rick's signature left-slanting scrawl immediately from a lifetime of sharing living quarters with my brother, the ultimate Corroded Corpse fanboy. Mass-produced centerfold spreads still hung on the walls of my house from various music magazines, photographs in full-color with signatures printed across them. Kevin had cherished them all as if they were personally inscribed. Rick's penmanship graced the liner notes inside the band's albums as well, from handwritten lyrics to clever hidden messages for the fans to find.

I peeked inside the envelope, and gasped.

Digger had some explaining to do.

I FOUND Adrian and Abbey in the kitchen. Breakfast was indeed in progress on the stove, but those two were conferring, thick as thieves, at the kitchen island. I glanced around suspiciously. Markers and paper were strewn everywhere. Adrian, leaning on his forearms across the work surface, hastily slid back and nonchalantly grabbed a spatula. Abbey curled her feet around the chrome rungs of the stool she perched on and quickly immersed herself in her artwork, pretending to whistle even though she hadn't quite mastered the skill yet.

"What's going on?" I demanded. "And why does everyone look as guilty as the proverbial cat who swallowed the canary .. . except for the cat?" Chelsea was hunkered by a tiny ceramic bowl, chowing down on dry food rather than the smelly, oily fish Adrian had joked about upstairs.

"Nothing," Abbey sang. "Just drawing."

"Abbey's been keeping me company while I was cooking, and now," Adrian sidled up next to me with frying pan in hand, "brekkie is served." He slid a healthy portion onto Abbey's plate, and she quickly abandoned her art.

"How come your eggs are so much fluffier than Mommy's?" Abbey demanded around a mouthful.

"Chew first," I advised her. "Ask questions later." My advice, of course, didn't apply to me. "Care to explain?" I asked, placing the envelope I had found next to the plate Adrian had just prepared for me.

"Ah, yes," he supplied, bringing his own serving to the island. "I was going to tell you about those."

"Adrian, these are tickets to the Library Lions gala! And it's tonight!"

My lover swapped out his potholder for my hand and twirled me toward him like we were on a ballroom floor. "Will you do me the honor?" he joked.

"These tickets had to set Rick back a bundle," I protested.

"He said his in-laws get an entire table at the benefit." Adrian gave a shrug and took me for another whirl in the opposite direction.

"An entire table?" I sputtered. Scoring two tickets to one of New York City's most anticipated social events of the year took big bucks; securing an entire table was probably equivalent to the GDP of a third world country.

"The perks of being a 'cultural conservator,' I reckon," he said with mock panache, and dipped me so low I squealed, sending Chelsea skittering right across the top of her food dish and out of the kitchen. Abbey grinned through a mouthful of bacon.

"Speaking of donating to the library," I chided, "I heard my local branch received a generous sum recently." The library director had asked me repeatedly to remind Adrian to cash the check cut for his services after he performed last April. No sooner had the check cleared than a donation was made, coincidently for that exact same amount. "Does that make you a 'cultural conservator,' too?"

"I'd prefer the term 'anonymous benefactor,'" Adrian allowed, smiling modestly. "Now, eat before your eggs get cold."

"I still can't believe this," I said, turning over the tickets to the iconic annual event.

"Why not? On our first real date, you told me you always wanted to attend one of their galas." He handed me my coffee. "One sugar, two splashes of skim."

"You remember everything, don't you?" I asked, with more admiration in my voice than accusation.

"The devil's in the details, darlin'." Adrian flashed me a grin and picked up a fork. "Or in this case, the devil on *this* shoulder plots diabolically, while the angel over *here*"—he patted his other shoulder— "dutifully takes notes."

Leaning toward Abbey, he stage-whispered, "The secret to fluffy eggs is . . ." He put the back of his hand up to his mouth as he delivered the rest of the message privately in her ear. Her big brown eyes widened.

"Mommy, you *really* need to put sour cream in *your* eggs," she dictated, both hands curling around the glass of orange juice Adrian set down in front of her.

"You're too much, Mr. Graves," I said lovingly, shaking my head.

"Come on, can't a rock star spoil his favorite audience of one once in a while?" he said, with cocky pomp and circumstance.

"Oh, so you call yourself a rock star now?" I tilted my chin up in challenge.

"Now and again," he quipped. "And last night? Certainly. But today . . . today is all about you."

~

IF THE DEVIL was in the details, I began to wonder how in hell I was going to be able to pull off a night out. Not only was it another school night, I didn't have a sitter for Abbey and had only brought one change of clothes.

"She's in kindergarten, luv. What's one more day? The absence won't go on her college transcript," Adrian teased as I voiced my concern.

"Yes, but—hey, don't try to ply me with bacon!" I protested, as he popped the last piece into my open mouth. "At the risk of sounding like Cinderella"—I tugged at the sash on the terrycloth robe I had appropriated from Adrian's bathroom—"I have nothing to wear to the ball."

A chime echoed through the spacious apartment.

"Batphone!" Abbey announced. Adrian's intercom system was accessible from any room in the house, but in the kitchen it was still connected to its original hardware: an old school, corded telephone, which happened to be red.

Adrian had it to his ear in seconds flat. "G'morning to you, Hector. Yes, you can send them both up."

"Company so early?" I asked. With Abbey in her footie pajamas and me in a borrowed bathrobe, we were the epitome of lazy houseguests. Our host, in a pair of beat-up board shorts and a hoodie zipped halfway up his naked, tatted chest, could at least pass for lounge-casual.

"No worries, Kat. They're family." Adrian smiled as Abbey's vinyl-bottomed feet hit the floor. Summoned by a sharp rap on the door, she shuffled out to answer it.

"Unkie Luke! Unkie Kimon!" Her squeal found its way back to my ears in the kitchen.

"Adrian Graves, what do you have up your sleeve?"

My lover turned his palms up innocently and his eyebrows followed, but his smirk was anything but.

Out in the foyer, Abbey was dancing on the shoe-tips of my brother-in-law. Unlike us, Luke looked dressed for the elements in jeans and a windbreaker, his ever-present backpack swinging casually from one shoulder. It no doubt contained one of his professional cameras, and other essentials for whatever adventure he had next on his list. His fiancé was dressed similarly, burly and beautiful, like he had just stepped out of an outdoor outfitters catalog. No surprise, as Kimon and Luke had met on a modeling shoot. Tucked under his muscular arm was a stack of papers, which he now bequeathed to Adrian.

"Beware of Greeks bearing gifts," Luke joked. "Thought we'd save you a trip to the newsstand today."

"Ah, my press awaits! Thanks, mate." Adrian eyed the pile with wary anticipation, as if it were a Trojan horse that had been pressed through a paper mill. Capable of surprise attacks.

"So . . . what brings you guys here?" I asked of the men I considered family. Adrian's impressive doorman building was hardly a "dropped-by-since-I-was-in-the-neighborhood" kind of place. Sure enough, the signature Lewis blush began to creep across Luke's cheeks. It was the same one that betrayed my late husband anytime he tried to keep even the most innocent secret from me. And on his brother, it extended up to the tip of his nose. It brought back a memory of watching the Lewis brothers lose spectacularly in a game of poker at a college party once.

"We're your fairy godfathers, Tree." My childhood nickname sounded foreign as it echoed through the hallway of Adrian's palatial apartment. But like the man who spoke it, not exactly unwelcome. "Here to take Abbey out for the day . . . and evening. Got your bag packed, kid?" Luke held Abbey at arm's length and twirled her, while she still perched on his shoes like a mini-shadow.

"Fairy godfathers, you say?" I raised a brow and shot Adrian a look.

"Bibbidi-Bobbidi-Boo, girlfriend," Kimon said in his Greek god baritone, and struck a pose with an imaginary wand in the air. "You know it."

I laughed. "Come on, Abb. Let's go upstairs and get you dressed and packed."

As she and I wound our way up, Abbey chattering a mile a minute, I heard Luke ask Adrian in an impressed murmur, "You have an *upstairs*?"

"Go brush your teeth, kiddo. I'll get all your stuff together." For Abbey, I had at least packed some additional changes of clothes, as accidents with a five-year-old were bound to happen. As I lay a fresh outfit out on the bed, something on her pillow caught my eye. It was a seashell, featherlight in my palm and just about the size of a nickel. I had never seen one so perfect before. And its color didn't look like anything found in nature, yet to the touch, it felt real. It began with a deep purple at its base, spreading to a bursting blue, and extended to the tips in a sea green, its outermost ridges highlighted in yellow.

"Abbey, where did you find this?" I asked, when she came trotting back in. She was, after all, staying in the room reserved for Natalie, and there were still many remnants of Adrian's daughter's rare visits left in the room. Like the Spice Girls poster, which I was surprised Adrian even let through the front door.

"Riff gave it to me."

Ah. I stroked the shell's smooth underbelly with my thumb. I now had no doubt it was definitely real. As everything I knew about Riff Rotten was painfully genuine.

"You mean Adrian's friend, Rick? When?"

Abbey shook her jammies off where they clung stubbornly

to her foot. "He told *me* to call him Riff." She sniffed importantly. "And he gave it to me last night, before the big concert. It's a moonrise shell," she added, "and he said they only grow in Hawaii."

I gave a soft chuckle, imagining shell farms under cool Kauai water and crops of these beauties. I never thought about shells growing before. But I guessed they grew from the bottom up, increasing with size as they added material to their margins. I contemplated that as I helped Abbey dress. "Can I bring it with me today?" my daughter pleaded. "For luck?"

"It looks like a pretty rare shell, Abb. I think you'd better keep it here, so you don't lose it. You can pack your new Max though. For luck."

Abbey gave a squeeze to the new plush replica of Maxwell MacGillikitty, her favorite cartoon cat, before popping it on top of her clothes in her little backpack and zipping it up.

"All set?"

Abbey slung her backpack on and quoted the feline private eye. "I'm prepared to do what ordinary cats won't do!"

"All right then," I laughed. "Be a good girl for the unkies, okay?"

"Will Chelsea be sad without us?"

Back downstairs, the tiniest occupant of Adrian's household was flopped, boneless and purring, in a spotlight of sun shining through the living room window. "The kitty will be fine. I'll make sure she is fed and cuddled in her bed in the library before we leave tonight, too."

The men were conferring in the foyer, and doling out handshakes. Had it really been four months ago that Adrian was willing to walk away from everything we had built at the mere assumption of a guy like Luke in my life?

He had of course assumed wrong, but only because I had built up walls and the memory of Pete until they loomed larger than the Cloisters tower, gray and severe. Adrian had had nothing to go on, except for the shrine of pictures haunting my house, and Luke was such a replica of his older brother that sometimes it was even hard for me to look him in the eye. Adrian had taken one look and convinced himself I was taking the safe way out, choosing caution over chaos by finding a more familiar specimen.

But as Pete had reminded me, in my most vivid dream of him, "there are all different kinds of love." As was evident from the glance Luke and Kimon shared as they stood by the front door, small smiles playing on their handsome mouths. And from the hug Abbey now hurled Adrian's way, as she prepared to say good-bye to him.

"You're not going away again, right?" she asked, her lip curling in worry.

"I'm not going anywhere," Adrian said, his clear blue eyes and grip on her bony shoulders just as emphatic as his tone. "Not anytime soon."

"Except to the ball with Mommy!" Abbey sing-songed, attempting a wink that caused adult laughter to erupt through the hall. I mouthed my thanks to my brother-in-law and future brother-in-law, as Abbey launched into a guessing game of where the trio was headed for the day. "I hope it's the Cloisters again, where the unicorn lives! And can we go to Cowgirl for lunch, pleeeeease?"

"I hope that wasn't too forward of me." Adrian closed the door and turned to me. "Finding care for Abbey tonight."

"Are you kidding? You placed her in the best possible hands."

"And what are you doing?"

There was amusement and desire lacing the lilt in his voice as I loosened the tie on his robe I wore, revealing my camisole and boy shorts. Their conservative, dark plaid pattern was unexpected in lingerie, and paired with black lace trim, made me feel like the epitome of sexy librarian.

"Now I'm"—I snaked my arms around his slim hips and pulled myself into his personal space— "placing *myself* in the best possible hands."

He laughed softly and slid his fingertips, warm and calloused from guitar strings, along my collarbone. Closing my eyes, I relished his touch as it lingered down my neck. His thumb found my throat's soft hollow, and a sigh escaped me. The thick terry of the robe slipped down one shoulder, and his lips fell on the skin exposed there.

For the first time in almost two months, we were truly and finally alone. His travels had taken him to L.A. to reunite with Rick, then back home but surrounded by a myriad of media and music people in preparation for the show. I had shared him with twenty thousand adoring eyes last night, but now I was ready to be his audience of one. Solo show. Standing room only.

I threaded my leg between his, inching my thigh closer to his growing interest.

"Easy, Tiger." His new go-to phrase echoed back to our first unforgettable kiss, as hazardous as it had been heady. He had, in fact, taken my words and debuted them to music last night. And now he fell back on them as I attempted to nibble away his resolve. "Not so fast."

"Mmm, but I want to hear you sing that to me. Now. Naked. In bed." With each command, I tugged gently at his lips with mine. "God, I'm demanding, aren't I?"

"No, not demanding." His reply fell softly against my mouth. "Deserving."

He wove his fingers through my curls, latching on tight to my kiss. One shift in his stance and he had me hitched higher, riding on his muscular thigh and grinding shamelessly against him. "Remember how I said today was all about you?" he breathed, reaching for the sash of the robe. He used it as leverage to pull me tighter against him. But in one deft move, he cinched it closed. "Sorry, luv . . ." The intercom bleated for attention on the wall behind him, and I heard the obnoxious follow-up ring of the Batphone in the kitchen. ". . . But I lied."

"NOT MORE COMPANY." I groaned and reluctantly slid my bare feet to the floor. The hardwood was a cold insult after the heat and magnetism that had molded our bodies together. "Ignore it. Send them away." But too late, Adrian had already taken the call.

"Yes, I've been expecting them. Thank you, Hector."

"Yeah, Hector." I pouted. "Thanks for nothing."

Adrian just laughed, and hung up the receiver. "You'll like this surprise, promise."

"Talk is cheap," I said, hands on hips. I didn't need any more deliveries: no more roses or surprise kittens or mystery tickets or fairy godparents of any persuasion. I didn't need anything else. Just him.

"Then no more talk for a while." His voice, along with the scruff of his goatee as he dipped to nuzzle where the robe met in a V, was rough. "Not when I'm paying these two by the hour." Adrian gave me no time to process his touch or his words before flinging open the front door. "*Hej*, Stefan! Sofie!"

Startling blue eyes met my gaze, under a swoop of white-blond hair. I don't think I had ever seen such a quintessentially beautiful human before . . . until his female counterpart stepped up and kissed Adrian on both cheeks. "*Tjenare*, Adrian."

Like the Eskimos and their numerous words for "snow," the Swedish couple Adrian introduced never repeated the same word twice, but they both seemed very happy to meet me. "*Morsning!*" Sofie clasped my hands warmly.

"*Halloj*, Katrina." Stefan pierced me with his eyes and spoke barely above a whisper. "*Roligt att ses.*"

"If it's all right with you, luv, I'll take Stefan." Adrian beckoned blithely. "It's been a while."

"Um, shouldn't we have . . . discussed..." I waved my hands between Adrian and the blondness between us. "Are we planning on an open relationship here, because I'm not sure—"

"Kat!" There was surprise and delight in his laugh. "They're professional. Licensed. Massage therapists. Masseur"—he nodded as Stefan moved past us with his portable massage table—"and masseuse." Sofie lugged her table in as well, and the couple began to assemble their tools over by the expanse of windows in the living room. "And yes, they're brother and sister as well."

I sputtered an embarrassed laugh. "You could've just said that before the doorbell rang."

"Yes, but where's the fun in that?" Adrian winked. He gave a slow stretch, and rubbed his lower back. "I'm not the young buck I once was. Playing a gig like that last night reminded me . . . 'twas murder on my back. Shoulders. Neck."

I wrapped my arms around him and moved my hands along each spot, in consolation. "You were amazing up there last night."

"I put on a brave front," Adrian gave a modest smile. "And I want to be amazing for you tonight, when you're on my arm. So . . ." He flicked off the lights and tilted his head toward where our makeshift day spa was waiting. "*Tjohej nu drar vi igång.* Let's get started, shall we?"

I grinned, adding yet another dialect to the growing list of languages Adrian spoke. "English, Portuguese, Icelandic, Swedish . . . what's next, Adrian Graves?"

"Wouldn't you like to know?"

A small folding screen allowed us to quickly strip down to our most comfortable state together. Stefan and Sofie had positioned the tables in such a way that we were able to hold hands, once we were settled in. Both therapists were experts at discretion, getting us swiftly covered as they began to work us into a more pliant and blissful condition than I even thought was possible.

I had a sliver's view of the golden park through the hole in the face cradle, thanks to Adrian's floor to-ceiling windows. To my left, my lover sighed as he slowly unwound under Stefan's bodywork. Adrian squeezed my fingers gently as Sofie performed a fluttering effleurage from my tailbone up to the wings of my shoulder blades. I felt absolutely buoyant, perched over the treetops, and Adrian's touch allowed my mind to sail.

"And to think you wanted me to send them away." Adrian's murmur morphed into a strangled, ecstatic groan. I could only imagine Stefan was putting the "Swede" in Swedish massage. And if his moves were anything like the cycle of rhythmic lifting, squeezing, and releasing Sophie executed, we both were going to be a puddle of melted muscle before the hour was up.

"Shhh, no talking," I mumbled, playing my thumb against his palm.

Sophie touched my shoulder lightly, her accent turning the words "over, please" into a sweet melody. She held the sheet taut as I flipped onto my back.

"You're so beautiful, Kat."

Adrian's whisper caught my ears, and I slowly opened my eyes to him. He was already supine, his gaze tilted toward me while Stefan stood above him and worked on his right shoulder and neck. Again, he caught my hand in a caress. I felt a shiver parade up my spine, even while it was pressed against the heated massage table. Sofie had worked her talented fingers into my hair and was massaging every worrisome thought I'd ever had out of my skull.

"Thank you," I whispered. It may have been meant for both of them, but it also could've been my message out to the universe at that very moment, or to myself, to remember, for all time. "*Tack*," Sofie whispered, resting her hands on my shoulders to indicate our time was up. I parroted her sentiment, not ready or wanting to move just yet. But since she had brought not only serenity but the massage table as well, I slowly relinquished my spot.

Sofie helped me slip back into my robe as Stefan dismantled the tables and packed up their supplies. Adrian was already back into his sweatshirt and shorts, stretching lean and languid. The scar along his tight abdomen moved with him, and the dagger etched above it appeared to quiver under the effort. A hot arrow of lust and longing surged to the bull's-eye of my sensitive center, sending vibrations outward. As if my legs weren't jelly already.

I hadn't wanted the massage to end; yet at the same time, I couldn't wait to get rid of any and all third parties.

"*Tack, tack.*" Adrian saw them to the door, their murmured foreign exchange following them.

"Oh my God," I breathed, collapsing against him after the door finally closed. "That was truly amazing."

He rolled his cheek against my temple, inhaling deeply. "You smell like a field of English lavender." Fingers found their way into my robe, loosening it, and fell against smooth skin. *Thank goodness for long couches*, I thought, as I pulled him against me and we landed in a tangle of sighing, smoldering kisses.

The warm oil had heightened the experience and our senses. Sharp citrus and crisp cedar met me as I tugged on the zipper of Adrian's sweatshirt, my hands sliding over his silky naked chest. It was a scent so different than his usual peppery aroma, yet just as exotic as it clung to his skin and gave his tattoos a vibrant sheen.

"Kat," Adrian gulped, and sprang up at my attempt to push

his hoodie off his shoulders. "Not here, luv. Poxy oil, it stains. Mind the suede."

I groaned, for once hating the supple, return-to-the-womb softness of Adrian's high-grade leather couch. It was of top quality, but seriously high maintenance.

If not here, then where?

"The dining room table could use a little polishing." I giggled wickedly as he hauled me back up into his arms. Just the thought of Adrian spreading me across the table like the most bountiful feast was enough to make me slicker than the massage oil had.

The Batphone trilled an interruption once again, and I practically screamed in frustration.

"Hold that thought."

"No, no, no!" I gave chase, through the dining room where the gleaming table for twenty mocked me, and into the kitchen. "Whoever that is, Hector needs to tell them to take a walk around the block," I advised.

Adrian bit his lip and raised a brow, like that was the most brilliant idea he'd heard all day. "How about you go up and start a long, hot shower for us? I'm right behind you."

"Promise?" I asked, but he already had his ear to the phone and a finger to his lips. Since when does a rock star shush a librarian?

Adrian Graves was definitely up to something.

I CONSOLED myself with the hottest shower possible. The multiple massage sprayers picked up where Sofie had left off, palpitating against my shoulders and back, while the huge rain-fall shower above washed away most of the oil and a tiny bit of the edge. Although if Adrian didn't join me soon . . .

I spied movement on the other side of the block glass that

curved around the doorless, luxury shower, and smiled. A flash of tattoos through the steam told me Adrian had kept his promise.

"You still smell like flowers," he said, gathering my wet curls in his fist like a bouquet. I gasped as his hardness met the hot, wet yield of my skin. "Told you I was right behind you." With a trembling sigh, he was in me; he was of me.

Reaching his free hand to strategically adjust the front sprayers, Adrian made me forget all about interruptions and Batphones. The pulsating water beat my body into submission, delighting spots he wasn't able to reach with his fingers, because they were busy elsewhere.

"I missed you so much." My head fell back against his shoulder, and he captured my mouth with his. Rivulets of water coursed between us, damming where our bodies locked before cascading over my curves with each of his slow, measured thrusts.

"When I saw you from the stage," he panted, "down in the pit last night, God, all I could think about was getting you alone. To touch you, feel you, be inside you."

"Well, you put on a brave front up there." I teased him with my tone and each pivot of my hips, but remembering the intensity of his playing stirred something primal in me. I wanted to be taken, in every way, by the guitar god who had stolen the stage, and my heart.

I whimpered and braced my forearms on the glass tiles in front of me as his teeth grazed my earlobe. I was on the edge of shattering but Adrian contained me. He kept me whole and moving with him, his hand splaying across my belly, fingers spreading skin made sensitive by his quickening thrusts. Until, with a shout and a scream, we lost ourselves. Lost control, lost track of where his body ended and mine began. He snarled and sighed as I quaked, tightening against him as he heated me from the inside.

"Holy amazing."

"We're pretty good at that, aren't we?" Adrian kissed a path down my back.

"Yes, but we suck at water conservation," I pointed out, passing the soap.

"We'll forgo a shower for a few days then, to assuage our guilt." He laughed. "So. More amazing than that massage?"

"Massage? What massage?" I reached for my towel and let Adrian take center stage under the rain shower.

"By the way, your brother and his new girlfriend are downstairs."

I froze, mid-twist in my towel turban. "What?"

Adrian poked his head around the corner of the block glass barricade. "Kevin." Shampoo suds dripped from his silver hoop earring and into his long sideburn. "And Liz. I told them to make themselves at home."

"While we were up here, making love?" I stammered. "I thought you were going to tell whoever it was to take a hike!"

"No, that was *your* idea. Brits are way more hospitable."

He hopped back under the hot spray, and I had half a mind to flush the toilet and ruin his good time. Instead, I pushed a rogue curl back under my turban, threw on my yoga pants, a T-shirt of Adrian's, and the most welcoming smile I could muster.

I'd show him hospitable.

"OH MY GOD, you guys! What are you doing here? Hi!"

Liz was lying on what had almost been the scene of Adrian's and my crime of passion. She had a magazine in hand, and the cat perched on her chest.

"I'm pretending I live here." She whispered, perhaps so as not to disturb Chelsea. Or lest my brother think she was bat-shit crazy. "Yep. This is my couch," she continued hoarsely, petting the gray suede, "and that's my park view."

I laughed. "Where's Kev?"

"I'm huddled in the corner with my hands over my ears, rocking myself and singing 'Happy Birthday' to drown out what I'm pretty sure I just heard," came a holler from the kitchen.

"Oh, gimme a break. The walls are thicker than that," I protested, but blushed all the same. "Back me up here, Red."

"I, the lady of the house, heard nothing." Liz perused her magazine like it was the most interesting thing on earth. "Maybe a little singing in the shower . . ."

"Whatever. I'm a grown woman. No need to justify anything. Especially not to you," I addressed my brother, "he who just did the walk of shame into this living room, wearing the same clothes as yesterday."

"I came to get your car keys, you bimbo. Since you stranded me here in town."

"Nice try, lamebrain." Liz threw the magazine at his head. "You weren't complaining about being stranded in my bed last night."

"Wow, three page spread! Killer," Kevin said. "Has Digger seen this yet?" He waved the magazine in my face.

"Has Digger seen what?" Adrian asked, slowly descending the spiral stairs. His hair was wet and slicked back, and he was slowly buttoning the sleeves of his black Western-style shirt. A flat brown paper bag was tucked under one arm.

I gauged my brother's reaction. Considering it had been less than twenty-four hours since learning his sister was dating one of his favorite musicians, I thought he was doing fairly well, keeping his cool. "*Manhattan Muse*'s write-up of the show last night." Kevin's hands, so self-assured in the kitchen, wavered slightly as he proffered up the magazine for all to see.

Manhattan Muse prided itself on the broad conglomeration of culture it presented to the masses on a weekly basis, picking up where *Time Out New York* and *Village Voice* left off. It could've either thumbed its hipster nose at the eighties doom metal band's resurgence, or dropped to its knobby knees in worship. But a three-page spread and a headline proclaiming THE BEAST IS BACK: ROTTEN GRAVES RESURRECTS THE CORPSE TO SOLD OUT GARDEN sounded pretty promising.

"Ace," Adrian commented, casting a glance at all the sources Kimon had brought that now covered the coffee table. The remnants of his *Clockwork Orange* eye had washed off in the shower, leaving just the material in front of him as hard evidence that the show hadn't been just some rock-and-roll fantasy we'd all imagined.

"I'll take a read-through after we eat. I'm famished. Can't imagine why." He aimed a wink my way. "When's lunch, Chef?" he asked Kev.

"Is that why you're here?" I wheeled around to face my brother, and then threw a glance at Liz. "And you?"

She was on her feet now, clicking a flat iron over her head like a belly dancer with castanets. "Makeover time, Tree."

Jeez, it seemed Adrian had enlisted everyone I knew. Was I that much of a charity case?

"So, do you have it?" Kevin wanted to know.

Adrian deposited the bag into my brother's waiting palm. "One mint condition copy of *Spoils of War*, on blue vinyl."

"Wait. You're bribing my brother with Corroded Corpse swag so he'll cook for us?"

"Very rare Corroded Corpse swag," Kev corrected, sliding the odd-sized record out of its sleeve to inspect it.

"Don't you trust me?" Adrian asked, amused.

"I trust no one," Kev reported ominously. "Limited edition, custom-shaped seven-inch single. For every one genuine copy, there are at least twenty bootlegged fakes." The serial numbers etched into the vinyl seemed to satisfy him, because he smiled broadly. "Lunch will be served in ten minutes." He trotted back to the kitchen, treasure in hand.

"I thought he already had that one," I whispered to Adrian. He'd done a quick inventory of my brother's metal memorabilia over the summer, convincing me to add a separate rider to my homeowner's insurance to cover it.

"No. He has the green," Adrian murmured. "Can't wait to see what I can get him to do to earn the red vinyl. Only fifteen pressed, and I know the whereabouts of exactly three."

Liz had me settle into the big leather chair in the corner, next to the end table where she had several hair appliances heating up. With all girls in the family, the Dooley household had been seriously into hair growing up; no shape, style, or tint had gone untried. Liz had done my hair on the first day of junior high, before prom, and for my wedding. It was only fitting, I supposed, that she work her magic now.

"I hope I'm not taking away from any time you and Kevin had planned to spend together today," I said, once Liz silenced the roar of the hair dryer. "Without going into gory details, how's it going?" Her fingers danced along a section of my curls, separating them from the pack and pulling them poker-straight between the tongs of the flat iron. A hiss of steam escaped.

"Your brother. Rocks. My fucking world."

I waited for her to throw out some sort of glass-half-empty statement about him living on the wrong coast, but it didn't come. "So glad to hear that, Lizzie!" Unable to bounce up out of my seat and hug her, I just grinned to myself. I felt her happiness radiate above me as she held my head steady and straightened another section.

Adrian kept us company, distractedly thumbing through the reviews. "'Shockingly potent' . . ." he quoted, ". . . 'impossibly flawless,' 'rollicking, galloping guitar-play . . .'" he tossed down one rag and laughed. "They make us sound like bloody Clydesdales!"

Kevin couldn't resist leaving his post in the kitchen to come hear his idol wax poetic on the concert reviews . . . or tossing in his own adoring two cents. "Dude, like . . . when you guys busted out with 'Plunder and Pillage,' I was as happy as a little kid with a birthday party at Medieval Times, man. So righteous!"

His fanboy fanfare had me laughing to the point that Liz had to stop working, for fear of burning my head as it bobbed with unbridled hysteria. She turned the threat of the tongs on Kev, to keep him from delivering his customary sibling knuckle punch to my arm in retaliation.

"I loved that you guys threw down that old school Judas Priest cover, too."

"Ah, 'United' wasn't planned; I had just teased the lick a few times during the course of the show, which prompted Riff to channel his inner Rob Halford." Adrian chuckled. "Then Sam and Jim just followed our lead."

As had the twenty thousand faithful. The sound of forty thousand feet, marching to the beat, had been jaw-dropping. I had no doubt the crowd, like little leather-clad lemmings, would've followed the band outside and marched right into the East River, had they been given the command.

"What's it feel like to have the world in the palm of your hand?" Liz asked; her eyes a glossy, moss green as she blinked them in Adrian's direction. Funny, this coming from the girl who wouldn't trust him as far as she could kick him six months ago. I know she'd been doing her best to protect me, and to lock up her own jaded heart from further hurt at the time.

Adrian narrowed his gaze to the pages in front of him, biting a smile back. "Madison Square Garden is hardly the world."

That's when I heard it. Not the weary modesty I was expecting, that normally came with talk of his band's once-upon-a-time world domination. No, there was a spark of something else in his scoff. *Like he'd just gotten the taste of a really good drug . . . again? And wanted more?* my brain suggested, but my heart sent a pounding summons for it to cease and desist in that line of thinking.

"Ah, listen to this one." He was holding up the *Muse*, unable to wait until after lunch, after all. "'Whatever deal Corroded Corpse made with the Devil years ago, it's clear the debt has been paid, and the Rotten Graves Project are worshipping kinder, gentler deities now. But don't let their age and smiles fool you. Digger Graves and Riff Rotten are still lean, mean, well-oiled rock and roll machines, and they completely decimated Manhattan last night.' Not bad, eh?"

His eyes scanned the rest of the article, before coming back up to the byline. "Alexander Floyd strikes again."

My ears pricked up at the name. The same rock journalist had written the article that had given me the final clues in my research quest to find Rick. And somewhere in the house, there was an entire book he'd penned on "the truth and turbulent times of Corroded Corpse," according to the subtitle. Adrian had called *Godforsaken* "unofficial, unauthorized, wildly inaccurate accounts published purely for monetary or shock value," but everything I had read by Alexander Floyd rang fairly true so far. "He's everywhere, isn't he?" I ventured.

Adrian ruffled the pages of the magazine. "He was there when we exploded onto the scene, and he was there when we imploded as well. And he's tried to sniff out every bone locked away in our closets of skeletons ever since. I believe we're some sort of pet project with him."

Thinking back to our game of Truth or Dare over the Memorial Day bonfire, and Adrian's humbling confession of the one person, alive or dead, he would like to meet and why, I realized I would like to get myself in a room alone with Mr.

Alexander Floyd, somehow, somewhere, to pick his brain. And perhaps get his prediction on what would be next for the most important man in my life, and his band.

"Hot damn, girl. Look at how long your hair is," Liz exclaimed. She offered me her handheld mirror and stood back. I took a look, to the left and to the right, at the silken caramel curtain that now framed my face. Normally my curly hair fell slightly past my shoulders, but straightened, I felt it rustle at the middle of my back.

Adrian was absolutely transfixed, the concert reviews forgotten. "Cripes, Kat."

"You like?" I asked, sending a swish over my shoulder in one sexy move.

"I . . . I . . ."

If Abbey were here, she'd say he was gobsmacked.

"He can't talk right now," Liz reported happily. "All the blood is rushing out of his brain and headed south."

"I adore you"—Adrian defied her claim, and his cheeks were a ruddy British red to prove it— "however you choose to look. But I must say, you look smoking hot right now. Especially whilst wearing my rock shirt."

I glanced down at his Dead Can Dream shirt and grinned. It was just a boxy black band tee. Liz grabbed a hunk of excess fabric at my waist and cinched it with a ponytail holder, allowing my feminine silhouette to shine through. Adrian swallowed noticeably and stood up, rubbing his hands on his dark denim-clad thighs.

"I'm going to go check on Kev's progress with lunch," Liz said pointedly. She raised a finger in Adrian's direction. "Don't mess her hair up."

I laughed as he captured my arms to inspect me at closer range. "If I'd known the effect it would have on you, I would've done it a lot sooner."

"No, no. No need," he murmured. "I love winding your curls

around my fingers. I love that they match Abbey's. This is nice, though, for tonight." He dipped his hand in, cradling the back of my head, then let the strands flow through his fingers like a waterfall. His other hand claimed my waist and slid up, tracing the outline of the band's logo where it curved along my chest.

"I was a dead man," he said, swallowing hard, watching his fingers move along the *D*. "I never dreamed you'd come along."

The kisses he dropped on my lips were featherlight compared to the deep, drenching ones delivered over my shoulder in the shower earlier, but just as potent.

"Chow! Now!" Kev hollered.

"I don't think your brother approves of me."

"Correction," I laughed, laying my hands on his cheeks, "he doesn't approve of me bursting his scuzzy teenage fantasy like it was a big, fat zit. The rock gods he worships are supposed to bag the hot chicks, so he, too, will bag the hot chicks in some sort of divine karmic reward for being a devoted follower. But if the rock god ends up with his sister . . . he goes straight to hell."

Adrian laughed all the way to the dining room. There was the mammoth table, set cozily for two with place mats kitty-corner. I had to bite back a smile, remembering how I had suggested an alternate use for the dining furniture earlier in the day.

Liz pulled my hair back with a clip like I was Sadie, her childhood cocker spaniel, always in danger of dragging her ears through her food dish. "Just in case," she said. "And I want to run the curling iron through and add some glam waves to it after you eat."

"Spa lunch is served." There was pride in my brother's voice as he plated huge salads for each of us, bursting with crisp, colorful vegetables and what looked like perfectly seared salmon on top. He had even made spiced walnuts for garnish. Roasted butternut squash soup accompanied the perfect fall meal. "Kev, you just whipped all of this together?" I marveled.

"Liz and I did some of the prep work at her place. But had I known there was such a stellar kitchen waiting for me . . . I woulda camped out in there all night!"

"You're giving me a complex, Underwood." Liz gave him a push. "Anywhere else you would've rather been besides my apartment last night?"

Liz had had some crap hands dealt to her over the years in the game of love. She'd learned to approach the table with a poker face, and she hedged her bets carefully. I could tell this was a heavy wager.

Kev scrubbed a hand over his white-blond spikes and grinned apologetically. Quicker than you could say "in the doghouse," he replied, "As long as you're with me? I don't care where I am." I saw the miniscule twitch of my good friend's lips before it ignited a full-blown smile. I mentally congratulated my brother . . . good to know he had some aces up his sleeve, and he wasn't afraid to use them.

"Come, sit. Eat with us," Adrian urged. The two didn't need to be told twice. Liz ladled soup, Kevin tonged salad, and pretty soon they were eating off each other's plates like newlyweds.

"I see you are serving healthier amounts these days," I ribbed. Back home in Portland, my brother doled out the best Lilliputian-sized fare around. And his restaurant's name, BITE ME, was his perfect retort to anyone who criticized his portion control. His concept was perfect for someone like me, who hated to choose. I could sample the whole menu and still have room for dessert.

"Ha, you sound like Dad. He called it 'stingy rations' when they visited in July." Chelsea gave a pitiful cry at his feet. "Come 'ere, Kitty Cat. I have some salmon in the kitchen for you."

"Let's not get her in the habit, Kev."

"Speaking of which, I was hoping to hear 'Habit' last night. And no 'Simone'? What was up with that?"

Adrian's eyes met mine above our soup bowls. For all

Kevin knew about his beloved band, there was still so much he didn't know, and might never know. Especially when it came to Simone. Rick wasn't ready to let the world pry into his loss just yet. And the fragile footing he and Adrian had established in their friendship didn't need the added strain of sore feelings, where "Simone" was concerned. Besides the band and their ex-manager, I might've been the only other person privy to the identity of its chief songwriter.

Adrian cleared his throat.

"What'd you think of the new song, Kev?"

"What did *I* think?" My brother was clearly thrilled to be asked. "Balls out, just about the best thing I've heard in a decade! Heavy, melodic . . . it had it all. Loved the guitar solo in the beginning."

"I'm all about new beginnings, mate." Adrian's legs twined with mine under the table, and his smile warmed me like the morning sun over Central Park had this morning in his bed.

Arise and drink your bliss!

The trill of the doorbell startled the soup right off my spoon. No intercom or Batphone preceding it indicated another tenant within the building had come to call. Adrian played footsie, his bare foot caressing my ankle, and made no move to get the door.

"Liz, would you mind getting that?"

She rose, slow and unsure, but assented. "No problem."

I watched her back. Kev watched her backside. Adrian's attention was back to his meal.

A shriek pierced the high-ceilinged foyer.

～

"MINDY CARMICHAEL! THROUGH YOUR PEEPHOLE!" Liz clutched her chest and reported back to us, like she was playing a jacked-up game of I Spy. "Even through a fisheye lens, she's gorgeous," she huffed, leaning against the wall.

"Mindy Carmichael," Kev mulled the name over. "Sounds familiar. Porn star?"

"Even better," I answered. "Reality TV star." Mindy Carmichael was part of the team who performed some serious magic on Liz's favorite show, *Makeover Manipulators*. How on earth did she know Adrian?

I had a feeling she wasn't here to borrow a cup of sugar.

"Well, don't just leave her standing in the hall!" Adrian rose to remedy the situation.

"Oops! Sorry," Liz peeped. She trailed behind him, and Kev and I brought up the rear.

"Hey, stud!" Mindy was into the apartment with a breeze of perfume that smelled like summer air.

As Liz had reported, gorgeous. And I would go one step further to even say luminous. Her heart-shaped face boasted eyes shining with inner joy. Each blue-black curl cascading down her back was perfectly formed and frizz-free. The dress she wore was Goddess-worthy, clinging and flowing as she glided in. "Terrific show last night."

"Thanks, luv. Come, meet my friends. This is Liz . . ." Liz gave a miniscule wave and I thought she looked ready to curtsy . . . or pass out. ". . . and Kevin . . ."

"You're . . . you're a Corpse fan?" My brother was captivated. After years of online chatting with other like-minded metal aficionados, the majority of whom were male and closing in on middle age, he didn't know how to take the creature before him. Had she even been born when the band formed?

"I'm no poser. My dad played their records all the time when I was little. There was no way we'd miss the opportunity to finally see a show together . . . and my favorite neighbor." Mindy grinned tiny pearls in Adrian's direction. "Oh my," she breathed. "This must be Kat." Everyone stepped away, and I felt exposed. "You weren't kidding about those eyes, Adrian. Emerald City!"

She clasped my hands in hers and said earnestly, "We are going to have so much fun."

Makeup hadn't been fun for me since the sixth grade, back when Marissa used to steal teal eye shadow from Colby's Five and Dime. We'd apply it way more liberally than necessary and vie for spots in the bathroom mirror to marvel over our transformation. After that, makeup became just another weapon in the teenage arsenal. Tucked into our Bermuda bags, right next to the emergency tampon and the Velamints.

I wondered if Mindy Carmichael had ever even had the need for a Velamint.

"We were just finishing up lunch," Adrian said. "Are you hungry?"

"No, no. You guys go ahead. I'm just gonna set up my stuff." Mindy hoisted a fist, and I realized she had brought her makeup kit, a black and silver-clasped affair only slightly smaller than Adrian's touring road case. *Holy cosmetology, Batman.*

My appetite suddenly diminished. Mindy Carmichael spent her days on *Makeover Manipulators,* transforming under-appreciated ugly ducklings before sending them off to huge reveal events: the high school wallflower turned into a blooming beauty just in time for her class reunion, for example. Or the black sheep of the family, groomed to gorgeous for the wedding no one expected her to attend. It was full of head-shaking, jaw-dropping, *holy shit* revelations. And tears. And craziness.

I was a little scared of what I had gotten myself into. Or precisely, what Adrian had gotten me into. Excusing myself, I pleaded full and thanked Kev for the amazing lunch, before ducking upstairs. I needed a few minutes and deep breaths to process. And I needed to brush my teeth, so I wouldn't exhale salmon on Mindy Carmichael as she worked her magic on me.

Hasn't this year been transformation enough? The woman in the reflection from the medicine cabinet mirror just raised eyebrows over tired, green eyes.

"You tell me," I said to her.

Parenthood had creased laugh lines into the corners of my smile and squint lines that I wouldn't trade for the world. But I'd be in denial if I didn't say the rigors of single parenthood had deepened them.

In my mind's eye, I saw Marissa at our weekly coffee conference last April, urging me to get rid of my marriage bed. Convinced that it was detrimental to my mojo, and that ditching it was the remedy. "One step at a time for this one," she had said. "First the bed ... then the *accoutrement*."

So I had moved, one step forward, one foot at a time. Donating the bed. Locating the singer my daughter adored to perform at the library. But then I had fallen swiftly for him. With Adrian, I hadn't been afraid to jump right in, feet first. Diving into his present, digging into his past, loving him . . . and finally allowing myself to be loved again. For who I was, for who I had been. For the here and the now.

"Thought we lost you there for a second." Liz joined me in the mirror, curling iron in hand. "You okay, girlie?"

I'd been focusing so much on my inner journey that I'd dismissed the outer one as frivolous. But now it occurred to me that our shells were important, too. The thought of Abbey's moonrise shell, given to her by Rick, surged to the forefront of my mind. Looking back, I'm sure it hadn't emerged that way, perfect, from the ocean. No, once it was dredged up, someone took the time to separate it from the others and wash the debris away, before going over it with the equivalent of a fine-tooth comb to reveal its true beauty and spirit.

"Yeah," I finally said, turning to her. "Just a little freaked-out by all this attention."

"Come on. It's not like there are any cameras or anything. She's just being a friendly neighbor." With a clamp of the curling iron, she began to attack my temporary, pin-straight tresses, adding wavy volume back.

"True," I admitted.

"You know what Marissa would say if she were here, don't you?"

"Um . . . she'd probably tell me to kiss her lily-white ass . . . and get mine downstairs in that chair." I smiled at the thought of my best friend, always telling it like it was.

"Exactly," Liz pressed, coaxing out another perfect ringlet.

"Do you think I need to manipulate anyone, or be manipulated, with all that makeup?"

"Trust the professional," Liz said. "Ow! Motherfucker." She jabbed her index finger into her mouth. "That burned. I should stick to making bagels."

I frowned, but a laugh also broke through. "Thanks for putting yourself in danger, at my expense. It looks great." I gazed into the mirror as she ran a wide paddle brush through the wiener curls she had created, and pulled a small can of hairspray she'd hitched in the waistband of her low-slung jeans.

"*Voilà!* And va-va-va-voom. You're one sexy bitch."

Downstairs, Mindy was waiting with her stash of womanly weapons. "Oh, jeez. We're not even going to need this." She tossed her eyelash curler back into her kit and gave me an envious smile. I think I liked her a little more already.

The clinking and spray of dishes being washed was our soundtrack as she began to prime my face. "Just us chicks in here," she murmured, dabbing here and there. "With the men in the kitchen . . . where they belong."

Liz laughed. "Damn straight."

"So, Kat. What are you looking forward to most tonight?"

Mindy twirled a long makeup brush, not unlike Jim twirling his drumsticks last night. She was a rock star in the world of makeup, and exuded a cool confidence as she got to work.

"I don't know," I said, wiggling my nose where the powder tickled me. So far, the Library Lions gala had been more an abstract concept than anything else.

I thought of its namesakes, Patience and Fortitude, holding stony court by the regal stairs. I imagined sophisticated food and soft lighting and a stellar Who's Who of the literary world partaking in drinks and dancing. But it was all just pale backdrop and props for a night out with my man. Plain and simple.

"Looks like we have no need for this, either," Mindy joked, tossing the blush she was about to use back into her case.

"She's already thinking about the post-*ball* activities, I'm sure." Liz cackled demonically. Mindy grabbed an angled brush and swept it through her bronzer with a grin.

"Very funny, Red. I'm excited for the entire night. But most of all, I'm looking forward to just being out with Adrian. He has this way . . . this way of insulating us, no matter how maddening the world gets." I thought back to the time he took me to that sold-out Dead Can Dream show at the Hammerstein Ballroom. Even when surrounded by thirty-six hundred headbanging fans, we had been in our own little world together.

"Yes, but that was before the world realized Tigger was Digger," Liz reminded me. She'd once referred to him as the bouncy cartoon character, due to the fact that, thanks to me, he had been hanging out under the radar as a highly entertaining figure to the sippy-cup set. "You may have to share him a little with the mad, mad world now."

Liz's words of wisdom weren't meant to smart, but the slow burn of them sunk deep and got me thinking. It was all fairy tales today, but what if Adrian went on tour? How could I deny him what he loved doing because of selfish fear?

I looked in the mirror and my heart shriveled. It had taken the intervention and kindness of a half dozen conspirators to get me looking this good, while nubile twenty-year-old fans with crow's-feet two decades in their future would be throwing themselves at Adrian every night on the road.

Mindy swooped in with shadow, so I tried to relax and let her brush away my negative thoughts. "I love working in jewel tones this time of year," she explained. "And you, my dear, are the perfect canvas."

"You know," Liz said, reaching to swivel up a violet lipstick. "I always thought Leanna would make a great subject for Mindy's show."

"Le? How so?" I asked, relieved to have a change in subject. Our friend had joined my, Liz's and Marissa's fab four posse in ninth grade, and was a petite Korean beauty.

"Admit it, she was an angry black swan in high school. Pretty, but she'd tear your head off."

I laughed at Liz's observation. "Leanna was a bit of a punk, wasn't she?"

"She's toned down the look, but her outlook still needs help. Perhaps if she had the master makeover manipulators on her side . . . ?" Liz shrugged and capped the lipstick once more. "Maybe she'd leave that sad excuse for a husband."

"I have a feeling it's slightly more complicated than that," I said. But thanked Mindy just the same as she passed us the business card for the show's producer. We chatted some more about our favorite episodes, and Mindy regaled us with stories from the inner sanctum of the television studio.

"I've got a tip to share," she said, staring into my eyes. I know she had to do that in order to smudge the perfect amount of eyeliner above my lash line, but it still felt like Mindy Carmichael was looking deep into my soul. "Channel your inner mermaid."

"My inner . . . say what now?" Here I thought she was going

to give me some top-secret cosmetic intel, beyond making a fish-face when applying bronzer, or refrigerating your lipstick.

"Think mermaid when you get in and out of the limo." A few more deep stares, a few more light strokes, and she stepped away to view her work. "The first time I rode in one, I ducked in headfirst. E! network had the red carpet exclusive on my big sequined butt." She laughed, twirling her eye pencil through the sharpener before using her hands for emphasis. "Not glamorous in wide-screen HD, believe me."

Up until that moment, I hadn't thought about a limo. Or much about a red carpet or cameras of any kind. Instantly, my palms began to sweat and my mouth dried to a pucker. "Thanks," I managed, as she began to prime and plump my lips.

"You've already got that mermaid allure going on," she added. She pressed her own lips together, prompting me to do the same.

"You think?"

"Totally. You've got a confident, beautiful energy. But you've got an alluring mystery about you, too. Very muse-worthy, Kat . . . with the emerald eyes." She gave me a wink.

It seemed Adrian's new song had yet another vote.

She pressed a tissue to my mouth, but instead of blotting, she dusted powder right on top of it to set the color, before whisking it away. "My little secret for perfect lips. Velvety and totally kissable."

"Kissable is crucial," I heard Adrian murmur.

"How long have you been standing there?" I demanded, smiling up at him. All he could do was raise his shoulders and hands in a helpless gesture and grin. Liz gestured for him to come closer, but he declined, claiming he didn't quite trust himself.

"We know Adrian has a weakness for sirens," Mindy referenced another of his songs with a wink. She gave a few more joyous sweeps of her big brush and stepped back for the last time. "I love using makeup to help transform a woman's attitude about herself. It's all about enhancing her natural beauty, and empowering her to embrace it. But you, sister." She shook her head. "You've been rocking it all along. Look at you!" She presented me with a mirror. My expertly made up eyes widened. She had played up all my strengths in ways I never could have. Coupled with Liz's dynamic 'do, I was certainly on my way to being red-carpet-ready.

"Thank" came with my inhalation, and "you" was exhaled happily. My eyes danced across all of their faces in turn, including my brother's, since he had finished kitchen duty and joined us.

"It was Mindy's idea," Adrian supplied. "I ran into her in the elevator the other day."

"Yeah, he was carrying his tuxedo from the dry cleaner's . . . and I had to ask what the occasion was. I figured he wasn't going to wear *that* on stage!" Mindy's teasing was affectionate and adoring, like a little sister's.

Adrian's eyes sparkled a blue patina. "So I told her about the Lions gala . . . and you."

I don't know if it was due to the fact that he'd written dozens of songs, but Adrian had a way of making the simplest of words convey multiple meanings. As "you" dropped from his lips, he breathed life and love into it, and made me feel like the most cherished object in the room.

Until Mindy's mention of the tuxedo sank in.

Adrian would be dressed to the nines, and I still had zero wardrobe possibilities that could begin to do this event justice. I thought back to my own closet, just about an hour's drive away. Past the piles of laundry waiting for me, I probably had two dresses from my B.C. (Before Child) wardrobe hanging in there that could pass muster: the teal dupioni silk bridesmaid dress from Leanna's wedding, and the black velvet cocktail number I wore way back when I accompanied Pete to that United Nations Association awards dinner. I wasn't even sure if either still fit me, and truthfully, I had no desire to ever don either of them again.

Adrian was eyeing me. Whether he detected my dilemma, or whether he had just been waiting to make the next move, I couldn't tell. But he bit his lip in anticipation.

"One more surprise, luv."

"Just one more? You sure about that?" Everyone laughed. "I don't know if my heart can take it." It was my attempt at a joke, but I was seriously *verklempt* at all their efforts. My heart filled to bursting.

"Come now," Adrian tilted his head toward the stairs. "You lot may want to see this, too."

THE FOUR OF us trooped after him, spiraling up to the second floor. My brother, who could never deal with heights or spinning, used Liz's belt loops for leverage, much to her delight. I followed behind Mindy, whose butt wasn't nearly as big as she made it out to be.

"Omigoddigger'sbedroom," Kev hissed in Liz's ear. I had to laugh. He had had a similar starstruck moment when we walked backstage last night and he had seen Abbey in Adrian's arms. Now I could see him pretending not to gawk as he scoped out the sleeping quarters of rock royalty.

At least I had remembered to make the bed.

"For she who claims she has nothing to wear to the ball." Adrian approached the closet.

Even Mindy, who had seen all levels of high fashion, gasped. Suspended within was an ethereal, frothy concoction of a dress. If I called it plain green, I would be lying, as its shades changed, from dark forest to a pale fern, with each fold and crease of the fabric.

"Ombré chiffon," Mindy surveyed with admiring, experienced eyes. "What an exquisite silhouette!"

Everyone murmured in agreement. Even on the hanger, you could tell it was designed to beautifully drape, crisscrossing in several ways to nip at the waist. It had a boldly cut v-neckline, but there was a crystal beaded bodice inset to fill out and flatter the plunge.

"You like it?" Adrian asked. "My housekeeper made it."

My jaw unhinged at the notion of sweet Ana laboring over what looked like a couture gown. "But . . . when . . . and how . . . and . . . ?"

Adrian chuckled, scratching modestly at his goatee. "The story starts with Natalie, actually. And September 11th. I never told you this, but she came to live here a few years back, and to attend FIT." Adrian's eyes clouded a bit as he brought up his only daughter. "Which was beyond huge, for her to want to come, and for her mother to let her. But then 9/11 happened, and yeah . . . she didn't want to stay after that."

My face fell in sympathy for him. He scrubbed a hand across his face as if to wipe the memory aside. "As soon as flights resumed, Natalie wanted me to take her home. I understood. But I was gutted. We were just starting to get comfortable with each other and I had high hopes. I wish I could have convinced her to stay. But at the time . . . it was all so surreal." Adrian cleared his throat, noting everyone was hanging on to each word of his story, enraptured. "So . . . about Ana. I came home one day to find her poring over the fashion textbooks Natalie had left behind. She thought I would be angry, since she was supposed to be cleaning the room." He shook back his shaggy hair and smiled. "I pulled some strings and she enrolled in Natalie's place that day. It's taken her a while, with the language barrier and whatnot, but no question: fashion—and talent—has its own voice."

I was speechless at the notion that Adrian had been an ongoing benefactor to this promising girl's education, and neither of them had ever said a word to me. "How long has that dress been hanging here? And how on earth would she know my size?"

"Ana just delivered it last night, while we were at the show. She'd been working on it day and night. It was actually part of her final portfolio project, so we'll have to make sure we get some good pictures." Adrian winked. "Oh, and Marissa may have helped a little with your measurements."

"That sneaky bee-ach!" Liz marveled. I smirked; of course Marissa would have. After all, my best friend had accompanied me on every one of my lingerie shopping expeditions since meeting Adrian, so she knew my measurements, right down to my skivvies.

"We need to get this on you." Mindy took charge. "Shoot, why didn't we think to have you in a button-down shirt? I don't want to mess your hair and makeup. Can we cut the shirt?"

"I'd rather you not," Adrian sputtered. "That tee is valuable vintage—especially now that Jim has joined *my* band!"

"Yeah." Kevin rose to back him up. "Like when Jason Newsted left Flotsam and Jetsam to play for Metallica. Think of the provenance! Cutting that shirt would be a sacrilege."

We paid no mind to their obscure metal references and shooed them out of the room. Liz helped me to carefully peel the T-shirt off; luckily its cotton had been washed soft and its neckline had stretched in Adrian's fondness of wearing it. Mindy held the gown, and all together, we bound me into it. It contoured my every curve, and I couldn't stop turning to the left and right in front of Adrian's full-length mirror. Its bold details and fluid lines elevated it to another level of stunning.

"That bustier really amps up the sex appeal," Mindy praised. "God, and look at that high slit in the front!"

I had noticed it too, and had sent my usual thanks to the gods above that I had thought to shave my legs that morning.

Liz sighed, fingering the fabric, and I followed suit. No matter how seductive and daring the cut, the lightness and softness of the material made it ultra-feminine and refined. It was perfect in every way. I loved the train, which was long enough to add glamour and sophistication, but not so impractical that I would trip over myself walking in it.

And speaking of walking, a pair of wicked-cool strappy heels completed the look. "No glass slippers for you," Liz dictated. "Those kick ass and take names. I'm so borrowing them when you are done."

"And I've got the perfect clutch for you to carry," Mindy said, manipulating buttons on her phone. "I'm texting my hubby to bring it over."

She pushed my chestnut tresses off my shoulders to play up the flattering straps of the dress and, after begging forgiveness for her familiarity, pushed my boobs up to defy gravity before adjusting the drape perfectly around the tight, sequined bodice. It was so sparkly; my décolletage really didn't need any other adornment.

"You ready?"

I nodded, and the men were let back in.

Adrian used no words. He strode right up into my personal space, and grinning, he took my hand and slowly brought it to his lips.

"Do you approve?"

"*J'adore*." His gaze lifted to meet mine, and indeed, the rest of the world fell away. "I adore." Heat began with a prickle at my toes in their sexy shoes, and radiated upward.

Kevin looked around the room, trying to figure out where

his sister went. Liz gave him a shove, and his smile finally came down to settle on me.

"Hey, everyone's giving you stuff, except your flesh and blood. I have something I want to give to you, too." He turned to the others. "We'll be down in a minute."

Adrian gave a nod and herded the women back downstairs.

Kev reached for his wallet—a long leather chain-and-clip affair like bikers wore—and began to rummage inside. "It'd better not be some expired condom from high school," I warned. My brother was known for crude sentimentality.

"Give me a little credit, sis." He rolled his eyes under their long lashes, and I had to. After all, he had been a lady killer in high school. I'm sure no condom in his wallet went unused for long.

"Just kidding. But really, you don't have to give me anything. You cooked all that spectacular food for us."

"Eh, food gets digested." His fingers found a small packet of tissue paper, and he flicked it open. "But diamonds? They last forever."

"Kev!" I peered at the sparkling bounty nestled in his cupped hands. "Those are Mom's teardrop earrings. How the hell did you get them?"

"Questions, questions. Such a burden." My brother shook his head.

"And answers are a prison?" I prompted, pinching an earring from his palm and leaning to put it on. His shock was apparent.

"You? Quoting Corroded Corpse lyrics?"

"When in Rome . . ."

"When in Digger Graves's bedroom," Kev murmured, lifting a hand for a high five. I scowled at him.

"Come on, Tree. I'm really stoked for you." His voice softened to a level very un-Kevin-like. "And I'm proud of my big sister today."

"For what? Going to a gala?" I tilted and secured the second earring.

"Pssh. No. For picking up and moving on. What happened to Pete . . ." he trailed off and chose a safer path, so as not to ruin my makeup or his reputation with tears. "What happened to your family would've flattened some people. I thought you were crazy, moving back home. But now I see . . . I see the steps you took, to make sure Abbey had a happy, safe life, and how brave you were. And strong. And I'm glad you not only waited for the right guy to come along, but that you took the leap when you found him."

He gave me the most careful bear hug, so as not to muss me.

"Thanks, bro. I'm proud of you, too. You've done amazingly well for yourself."

Kev broke away from me and jammed his hands into his jeans pockets. He turned his ankles out in his Doc Martens, and I had a feeling it was confession time. "PDX is getting a little played out."

"Seriously? But the restaurant—"

"BITE ME is still doing well. But there are new trends taking over the Northwest quadrant. And man, until I woke up in Manhattan . . . I had forgotten how much I loved this city."

"And . . . ?"

"And Portland chicks are cool, but I missed girls like Liz." I raised my brows higher, and he surrendered. "All right, all right. I missed *Liz*. Okay?"

I nodded. "She's all kinds of awesome, isn't she?"

"She's . . ." Kev rubbed the back of his neck in thought. "She's a hell-raiser and a godsend." His voice dropped an octave. "I should've been worshipping her all along, Tree."

It was my turn to throw arms around him. "Mi casa es totally su casa, you know that, right?" My parents had bequeathed the house to me, but only because I was geographically present at the time. "The boogeymen room is still intact, and it's all yours."

Kevin laughed at the nickname Abbey had given his teenage shrine of a bedroom, with its wall-to wall metal posters and memorabilia. "It's not a one-hundred percent done deal, so please don't say anything to Liz. Or, God forbid, to Mom." Our mother was going to have a complete conniption if both her children were on the same coast as her. "She left her earrings behind when they were visiting for the Fourth. I'm sure she'd approve of you wearing them tonight. I was instructed to give them to you, since you'd be seeing her soon."

That was right, Thanksgiving was less than a month away. My parents would meet Adrian for the first time. And he would have his first proper American Thanksgiving that wasn't served in take-out containers. I couldn't wait.

But I still had an enchanted evening to get through, first.

We wound slowly down the spiral stairs, and the sight I was met with almost stopped my heart . . . and kicked my ovaries into high gear.

"Nice to meet you, mate," Adrian was saying to a tall gentleman, who I assumed was Mindy's husband, in the doorway. "And this must be the wee Liam!" He reached for the baby with zero hesitation and such confidence, that the little boy had no qualms leaving his father's arms.

"Lars brought over the purse I wanted to lend you," Mindy said, introducing us, "along with my little teething monster. Thank goodness he's almost weaned." She threw her arms protectively over her ample breasts and laughed.

Watching Adrian bounce the baby in his capable arms sent a surge of love through me. I wondered if Natalie was the last baby he had held. Even after two decades, he didn't seem rusty at all. Abbey hadn't breastfed in almost four years, but I could practically feel that phantom tingle. The baby gummed at Adrian's collar, dampening it with drool, but my lover just laughed, and placed a gentle kiss on Liam's downy blond curls.

A lightning bolt of longing hit me. Could this be in the cards for us, a few years down the line? That was a lot of cart before the horses . . . but not so far outside the realm of possibility. Liam, the little social butterfly, reached for Liz next.

"Do you want to hold him?" My friend tested Kevin with a golden gleam in her eye.

"Um . . . no thanks. Babies are like that one ingredient I never know what to do with," my brother admitted, shuffling his feet in his Docs.

"Oh, yes," Liz cooed. "Like a little kohlrabi." She cradled Liam's perfect head.

"We'd better get him down for his nap," Mindy said, gazing adoringly at her son.

"Oh, before you go . . ." Adrian nipped into the library and emerged again, a few CDs in hand. "Signed copies for your dad, Mindy, and one for you and Lars as well."

I spied my pocketbook near the door and rummaged through it. "And for Liam," I said, handing over a third disc. Abbey and I were never without a copy of *Songs for Natalie*, the album that fate had placed in my hands many months ago. "Perfect lullaby tunes. Thanks for everything, Mindy. And for lending me your evening bag. I will return it, first thing tomorrow morning."

"Or second. Or third." Mindy winked, and gestured for Lars to grab her makeup case. "I know how it goes when you have a sitter for the night." She turned to Adrian and patted his cheek. "Let me know when you book your world tour, Stud. I'll come in and water your plants while you're gone."

World tour?

My feel-good fullness was robbed and replaced by a barren emptiness.

"We'd better get going, too." Kev hoisted his bag of catering supplies in one hand, and took Liz's with the other. She had her bag of hairdressing tools on her shoulder as well. "Leftovers are in the fridge."

"Have fun, you crazy kids." Liz blew us a kiss, and as Adrian closed the door behind them, I knew we were once and for all, finally and truly alone. And it was high time we had a serious talk.

"MINDY WAS JUST JOKING about all that, wasn't she?" I blurted.

"Of course. You know I have no plants." He gave a cheeky grin as he checked his watch. "Cripes, we'll be late for the ball."

"Adrian . . . I'm serious."

"I am, too." His steady gaze into my eyes suggested we'd have all the time in the world to discuss the matter . . . some other time. "I'd better get ready. Give me ten minutes, luv."

"Ten minutes? Jeez!" And here it had taken all day for me to get presentable. "You've got it easy."

Adrian laughed. "Okay, maybe fifteen, tops. It is a big occasion, after all."

"And after all this fuss," I said, unable to bring myself to look him in the eye, "are you going to want to hang around the ordinary, everyday Kat?"

"I'm having trouble hanging around you now, and minding my manners." He kissed me in every acceptable and available place that hadn't been primped and pampered. "You are a vision, now . . . and always. There is nothing ordinary about you, Kat Lewis." I shivered as a kiss landed behind my ear, and then dragged to the nape of my neck. My fingers fell upon his collar, which was still damp from baby Liam's affections, and I felt tears prick behind my eyes.

Let's not think about tomorrow, I heard his voice tell Abbey earlier.

Adrian was stalling both of us.

He bolted up the stairs, two at a time. Sighing, I gathered the essentials I'd need for the evening. Mindy's clutch was indeed perfect for a night out with my British hard rocker: a small black leather hard-shell, with tiny grommets detailing a pattern of the Union Jack. But its best feature was the combination clasp and handle, which looked like a set of brass knuckles, perched right on top. They were adorned with large, blingy diamond-like stones, and skulls with glittering rhinestones for eyes. As I slipped my phone and wallet in, I noticed Mindy had left a little gift of emergency lipstick in there for me.

Upstairs, I made one quick sweep of the bedroom to make sure I hadn't forgotten anything. Ah, tissues. With my luck, I'd probably get choked up with tears at some point in the evening to come, and would need a few.

"Luck" reminded me of Abbey and her shell. I plucked it from her pillow and studied it. The thought of Rick plying my daughter with such a present got under my skin and irritated me. Was it—and were the gala tickets—just some consolation prize, mementos to remember his bandmate by when he whisked him off on some twenty-date tour? I nestled it into the tissue before popping it in my purse. I planned to confront Rick about it.

And besides, I could use all the luck I could find.

Chelsea sat at the bottom of the spiral stairs she had not yet learned to climb, mewing hunger. I scooped her up and got her settled in her cage in the library, complete with fresh, dry food and her litter box. She kneaded happily at her little bed with tiny paws as she made herself at home. *I guess I should be doing the same*, I thought, glancing around. I hadn't been in the room of floor to-ceiling bookcases in a while. Impulsively, or perhaps compulsively, I searched the shelf for the last reading material I had perused, and there it was. On the same shelf, as if it hadn't been touched since.

And maybe it hadn't.

I pulled Alexander Floyd's *Godforsaken* biography out, flicking on a brass table lamp as I passed it, and settled carefully in my dress on one of the brown leather couches.

If I was to see Rick tonight at the gala, I wanted to be a bit more prepared with my secondary sources. Adrian's stories, as intimate as they were in their details, may not have been the most objective, understandably.

"Ach, Kat. Really?" I glanced up to find Adrian hovering in the doorway. "My word isn't good enough for you?"

Everything about Adrian was good enough for me. Handsome didn't even begin to describe how he looked, dressed for the gala. His tuxedo was all crisp lines, and contoured his lithe body like only a custom-fit could. I loved that he had accented it with tousled locks and a touch of scruff. "Of course it is. But pictures are worth words as well, no?"

Adrian couldn't suppress his smile. "If we're talking blackmail, some of those pictures are priceless." He shook out his sleeve and checked his watch. "We've got a half hour to kill. I could think of worse ways to spend it."

"Or better," I laughed as he collapsed onto the couch next to me. "But since we are all dressed up with somewhere to go . . ."

OUR KNEES BECAME a book rest as I propped it open. "I want to get to know Rick a little better."

"Well. I knew Rick, pre-Simone," Adrian said, licking a thumb and pushing past the first few pages. "And then of course, there was the Simone phase itself. But I'm afraid I know about as little as you in terms of post-Simone Rick."

The band's wantonly public mouthpiece had become intensively private since sequestering his family in Hawaii. Rick had been harder to track down than Adrian, and with good reason.

Caregiver to his wife as cancer quickly claimed her, then sole parent to three teen boys, were not exactly roles in keeping with the singer's once infamous persona. Had performing last night been a mindless flick of the switch for Rick? He'd made shifting gears after so many years look effortless.

"I'm curious to know what made you guys tick."

"Oh, we ticked, all right. Like a bloody time bomb." Adrian flashed a wry smile. "Luckily, I've got a much longer fuse these days."

He chuckled to himself as we turned to a fuzzy black-and-white class photo of Rick and Adrian in their Ditcham Park school uniforms.

"Aw, look how cute you guys were!"

"Cute?" Adrian protested. "We weren't aiming for cute. We were two guys aiming for total annihilation of our country through rock and roll."

He smiled fondly at the photo of the starry-eyed best mates. "We had to learn how to play first, though. I found a beat-up acoustic that had belonged to my stepfather and I began to teach myself notes and chords. Rick fancied himself a singer, so he worked on poses and struts when he was not doodling elaborate logos for the name we had chosen: *Diabolus in Musica*." He used air quotes and a deep voice, laughing at its ostentatious ring. "We had come across the Latin term in our school encyclopedia." My fingers ghosted his as they skirted down the glossy page of text.

Rick was summoned to spend the holiday with his parents in New York in the summer of 1977, which proved to be a long but evolutionary summer for both lads. Digger spent his break back in Portsmouth, where he could come and go without much hassle from his dad, and get reacquainted with his old friends.

"Good God, look at me and Sam!" Adrian pointed to a full-color photo of an adolescent version of himself and a chubby, grinning blond boy.

Sam Summerisle was a mate of the highest order; not only had he given Digger his nickname long before, he also freely offered up his sister Tess for snogging. Adrian received his first kiss that summer behind the motor mechanics garage where both their fathers worked. Sam, too, was hot to be in a band; his father had put him to work in the auto shop that year earning a few quid a week to save towards an instrument. Digger followed Sam's lead, working under his father at the garage until it was time to return to his mum's to prepare for school. He promised Sam that as soon as Rick returned, they would have Sam up for a proper band meeting.

"So what was Rick up to all summer in New York, while you were back home snogging?" I teased.

"What *didn't* he do? He sent many letters home, for one thing. Shared stories so incredible they were almost not to be believed, but it was New York City, after all. Anything was possible! Catching a Ramones show at CBGBs, seeing Debbie Harry walking down St. Mark's Place wearing pink sunglasses in the rain. Going to the Waverly in Greenwich Village at midnight to see *The Rocky Horror Picture Show* and throwing toast at the screen. Toast!" Adrian dreamily ticked off the list, his mind time traveling back. I pictured him as a teen, holding these letters, the ink smudging under his hot thumbprints with his burning desire to jump in and live within their pages.

"But it was Rick's final letter home that left me gobsmacked. A single word, written in red on one of those thin, pale blue airmail sheets: '*SHAGGED!*'" Adrian hoisted the book up to his lap again. "Ah yes, here's the picture he'd sent home." I peered at the scan of a bent Polaroid picture, depicting Rick and a black-haired beauty with cavernous blue eyes. "Rick had met a girl; a sixteen-year-old Manhattanite named Simone. Their parents had mutual friends in the same social circles. It was Simone who took him to the East Village, to the movies, to concerts . . . and ultimately to her bedroom on the Upper East Side."

Adrian shifted his weight, and glanced at me. "It was yet another case of the Have and the Have Not. Yet this one bothered me more. I could accept the imbalance of material possession. Yet in affairs of the heart, I was still standing on the outside with my nose pressed against the glass, looking in while Rick was handed tail on a silver platter."

Adrian turned back to the book with renewed interest, perhaps eager to change the subject. "Anyway, Rick came home soon after, with a 1964 cherry sunburst Gibson that his parents had bought for him in New York. He thrust it onto me so I could have a go, complaining of the blisters on his fingers from trying to play it. And so began my own torrid affair."

I rested my chin on his shoulder and followed along with his index finger.

Rick was lovesick and brooding over Simone. She had two more years left at Brearley before college, when she hoped her parents would send her abroad and into Rick's waiting arms. He went through a brief black turtleneck and poetry-writing phase, which Digger took the piss out of him for. "He'd ask me how my mate Simon was, and I would call him a cunt and tell him to fuck off!"

"Adrian! That wasn't very nice."

"It was for his own good! I told him no self-respecting woman was going to date a 'big girl's blouse,' and he needed to turn his depression into the heaviest music possible. So we vowed to make it our single-minded mission at the expense of everything else."

> Singing the blues helped Rick hone his vocal skills. Once school commenced in the fall, he signed up for voice instruction there to further improve his range. The lads began to write their own songs, but it was evident that they would need more manpower to bring it home.
>
> As promised, Digger invited his childhood mate up. Sam brought two things to the table: a crap copy of a Fender Precision Bass that he had bought for forty quid, and transportation. He and Rick, however, were as different as night and day, and butted heads routinely.

Adrian tapped an early picture of their trio, making music with a tiny amplifier and big hair. "I was constantly working as peacekeeper between those two. They were my two best mates so it drove me mad that they refused to take a liking to one another."

"What did they fight about?"

"Cripes, more like what didn't they fight about! They argued over football, television, the name of the band. Sam thought *Diabolus in Musica* was too fancy, too difficult to pronounce. He fixated on another name, Black Leather Fantasy." Adrian chuckled. "Rick would take the piss out of him, even after we had sold a million albums and were selling out arenas. If Sam got angry about something and threatened to walk out, Rick would have a laugh and ask, 'You going off to form Black Leather Fantasy, then?' Sam wasn't the brightest bulb. But he was a solid bloke and he really could play. Rick tolerated him mainly because it would be another two years until either of us could drive and it wasn't like Rick's aunt Bootsy could haul our gear in her Karmann Ghia."

More pictures had been unearthed of the two best friends.

Adrian, slight and fair, gold guitar in hand, gesturing toward the pickups on a V-shaped guitar strapped to the tall, lithe body of swarthy Rick. "Crikey, how he could shred on that Flying V! That's how he earned his nickname: Riff."

The "posh Jew" and the "puny pleb" were routinely bullied. Rick was called a Zionist, simply due to the fact that his father often had business dealings in Israel, and Digger was guilty by association, plus he wore the wrong brand of trainers. They were beginning to see how the world wasn't going to do them any favors. They were going to have to squeeze their own lemonade from the sour lemons life was pitching their way.

End of term came at Christmastime and once again, Rick was whisked off, this time for a skiing holiday in Switzerland. Sam was working two jobs back in Portsmouth, at the garage and unloading freight at the docks. Digger picked up enough hours as his father's apprentice to finally purchase a quality guitar of his own; a Gibson Les Paul Goldtop.

"My favorite. It cost me two hundred pounds, and I still use it to this day. My father thought I was daft to spend that amount of money on a 'hobby,' and my mum, well. Let's just say that her son's dreams of becoming a musician were not welcome dinner conversation. She wasn't convinced that playing music could provide a living or a pension. So when I told her, over the roast tatties, boiled sweets and Christmas crackers, that I didn't give a toss; I had decided to leave school anyway, she kicked me out of the house to help me on my way."

"Oh, sweetie. Where did you go?"

Adrian slapped over to a new chapter entitled "The Portsmouth Years."

"I went back to my dad's. He was a stern taskmaster at work, so for two years I was his whipping boy. But I had a goal; I wanted to be in London by the start of the new decade and playing music full time. So I kept my eye on that. I bought a small practice amp with my wages, and began taking lessons."

"And what about Rick?"

"Leaving school was out of the question for him."

Certain things were just expected of Rick, and academics were nonnegotiable. So he would put in a full day at Ditcham Park, and Sam and Digger would travel up from Portsmouth afterwards to clock in rehearsal time. But it wasn't all schoolwork that occupied Rick's day; he commandeered the pupil payphone to arrange gigs, mostly Bar Mitzvahs and parties where they would play original songs if tolerated and cover songs if requested.

"We weren't picky, we'd jump at any chance to play live. I think we even played at a hen night . . . what do you call them here, a bachelorette party? Yeah, for one of Bootsy's friends."

"*Diabolus in Musica* at a Bar Mitzvah?"

"Oh, back then we changed our name more often than we changed our pants! We were *Rue Morgue*, like the Poe story . . . then *Howler*. Oh, and *Houston to Delancey*—I think Simone had come up with that, she was always writing letters to Rick with suggestions for improving the band. Trying to make us avant-garde. For a long time we were called *Fetish*. Probably Sam's contribution, can't remember."

Adrian turned the page. "Ah yes. Cue the lovely Simone. She arrived the fall of that year to study at Queen Mary University. Straight from New York's Upper East Side to London's East End, but that didn't seem to faze her. She fell right in with us. Adam had joined as our drummer, and we had moved to London by then. Rick's parents funded a flat for us, so long as Rick enrolled in University there."

"So were you officially Corroded Corpse by then?"

Adrian nodded. "We were hanging out in the flat, drinking and listening to records, when Rick picked up the cover to Iron Maiden's brilliant debut. He gestured to the artwork, which featured a gape mouthed zombie-like creature, and scoffed that we could do better than some corroded corpse on our album cover. We all just looked at one another and it clicked."

So with the name and lineup firmly established, and shortly thereafter a demo under their belt, the band began playing regular gigs around London, gaining an impressive loyal following of denim-clad teens, their leathers covered in badges and pins to prove their allegiance to the various bands of the era. The U.K. youth in the London heavy metal scene were a recognizable force by 1981. In fact, there wasn't much difference between those on the stage and those in the audience. Digger was 18, and knew the ins and outs of almost every club in town as both a musician and a concertgoer. His reputation led to secondary jobs as a stagehand and guitar tech at larger venues like the Marquee and the Rainbow.

"Were you a roadie?" I asked him.

"I was more like local crew for the clubs. Not only did I get to see a ton of quality shows, buckshee and front and center, but I also met a lot of musicians, managers, and A&R blokes from various record labels. Every connection was a step closer to discovery. But it was a chance meeting in a pool hall that led us to our manager."

The edge in his voice was palpable. Several of the book's glossy pages crumpled beneath his death grip. I smoothed my hands across his, soothing as I moved up his arms.

"It was Wren who suggested Rick shorten his somewhat 'ethnic' surname to Rotten. When we moaned that it sounded like a blatant rip-off of the Sex Pistols' Johnny Rotten, Wren pointed out, 'Do you really think Chaim Witz would have gotten very far leading KISS?' See, he just knew all these bizarre rock facts, like Gene Simmons's birth name. He could recite how many albums a band had sold or what a venue's capacity was without batting an eyelash. And when that eighty-page contract from the label was couriered to our doorstep, he was able to offer up valuable points of advice, like 'Get a feckin' lawyer so we can sign this thing!'"

"Wow. How did your parents . . . and Rick's . . . react?"

"Rick's parents had been ever-supportive of us, so long as Rick continued with school. They always expressed interest, even attended shows when they could. I hadn't seen either of my parents since moving to the big city." He waved his hand to dismiss the memory. "I couldn't be arsed; I had a contract with my name on it! We took it straightaway to my brother, who was in law school. We didn't exactly have the money to put a professional on retainer, or the foresight to have Wren's own deal examined at the same time, unfortunately. But Michael did all right by us. The most important revision he made, and to this day I am in his debt, was to stipulate that ownership of the masters from both the EP and from *Ruins of Decay* be retained by the band."

"Why was that so important?"

"Well, when a band breaks big, often several albums into their career, their less-commercially successful back catalog increases in value. It was money that Wren could never touch, no matter how big he made us."

"Ah, gotcha."

"Our contract was a five-album deal with two firm, and the label was hot to get the band in the studio. Recording near home rather than being on the road fit in perfectly with Rick's schedule, as he and Simone had—surprise!—a baby on the way and a wedding to plan. The elder Rottenbergs were none too pleased."

"Didn't they care for Simone?"

"Oh they were very fond of her, but once they learned Rick planned to juggle the band, the books, a wife *and* a child . . . they knew something was going to give, and from the looks of things, it wasn't going to be the music."

"Oh man. How old were they?"

"Simone was twenty. Rick, going on nineteen."

"Her parents must not have been too thrilled, either."

Adrian shook his head. "But Rick and Simone were in their own little bubble of bliss and refused to let anyone pop it for them. That's how things were, back in those days. Me and you and let's shut out the rest of the world. Until, of course, contractual obligations forced us to tour in support of the album, ad nauseam. None of us saw our families much that year."

I turned the page and was surprised to see one of Marissa's favorite bands during her high school years.

When the band returned home to London, they learned that while they had been out playing some of their best shows yet, another British band was sashaying through the living rooms of America.

"Whoa, what are they doing in your story?"

"While Corroded Corpse really didn't care what Def Leppard was up to musically, we were intrigued by America's reception of them via a new channel called Music Television."

"Ah yes. I remember them entering my living room." I giggled. "My friends and I would rush to my house after school to watch hours of MTV."

"Ach, probably the worst thing that ever happened to rock and roll. Personally, I'd rather watch wallpaper peel. So yes . . . Def Leppard. We didn't give a toss. But Wren had a way of making us feel we had to. He dangled their *Pyromania* in front of our noses like a carrot. And vowed that if we stuck with him, it would soon be *our* album on the turntables of every teenager on earth."

He flipped to the back of the book, revealing a full-color photo of the band labeled "Rock in Rio, 1985: 350,000 strong." Leather-clad, sweating and screaming for the crowd that spilled well past the recommended bleed lines of the glossy page. Adrian slowly shook his head, as if he could scarcely wrap it around the notion. "And well . . . you know the sordid story from hereon."

"Yet here you are."

"As are you." He smiled and caressed my knee. "Your chariot awaits."

ONE SPELL WAS BROKEN, yet another began as Adrian's doorman ushered us through the heavy brass entryway of his building. Manhattan was alive at street level, the night's pace frantic in every direction. Headlights swept north and south, and to the east loomed the dark leafy wilderness of Central Park; the valley I had stared down at from high windows today was now a backyard filled with secrets.

Mixed feelings slowed my steps. Was all this fuss just preparation? Adrian buttering me up, just to tell me he was leaving for another two months? He had talked of longer fuses . . . had a new countdown to detonation already begun?

"Would it be silly to suggest changing into sweatpants and ordering in Chinese food instead?"

Or would it be delaying the inevitable?

"Come on, now. My Cinderella isn't getting cold feet, is she?" Adrian asked, a west wind tousling his hair against mine as he turned to face me. "That's not how I recall the fairy tale going."

"There's that "f" word again."

He laughed. "Just enjoy it, luv."

"While it lasts?" I added. Had he planned this whole fairy tale evening because he was going to be on tour and we weren't going to have many nights like this together anytime soon?

He smiled, and it hurt my heart to think it.

Our limo was waiting curbside, its glossy black exterior blending in with the night. Adrian chauffeured me right to the open door. Remembering Mindy's words, I plunked down, ass-first, and swung my legs in. I heard pleasantries being exchanged between him and our driver as he walked to the other side and climbed aboard. Soon we were sailing past Columbus Circle, sealed in our luxurious surroundings.

"Funny, I feel like we've done this before," Adrian gave me his cheekiest grin.

"Yes, I remember it like it was yesterday," I joked. It was hard to reconcile the man in the bespoke tux sitting beside me with the leather-clad, sweaty rock god who had brought an entire crowd to their feet and then down to their knees in worship last night. I fingered his bowtie, appreciating that he had taken the time to hand-knot one, rather than opting for a premade clip-on that would have cheapened the look. "You clean up nice," I added.

Adrian's laugh was lost to the night air as he opened the moonroof and leaned back. The neon dazzle of Times Square lit his eyes like a marquee on opening night.

"I love you, Kat Lewis. You absolutely rock."

His lips lingered near my earlobe, adorning it with words so beautiful and polished, my glittering teardrop diamond earrings had competition. About how stunning I looked, not just now, but this morning, as I slept. And how he felt he could conquer the world with me on his arm and by his side. Not to mention he was thinking of violating me six ways to Sunday in my fancy dress. All delivered in that flowing, murmur of an accent; it was enough to make me want to scream "Home, James!" to our driver and let the gala tickets go to waste.

"Promise me I can mess up your makeup later," he breathed, his hand spanning from my chin to cheekbone with a barely there touch that left me straining to meet him. "After we've hobnobbed with the literary elite."

My own hands drifted, mingling with the long locks that rested against the peaked lapels of his tuxedo jacket. Under the grosgrain tailored threads and crisp, spotless shirt, a colorful wilderness awaited me that I longed to explore, leaving lipstick kisses along every path to mark my way. Or to lose myself completely. "I promise," I whispered, and made a silent vow to myself to stop worrying.

"Right, here we are, then." The limo had glided past the cross-streets of 42nd and Fifth, the epicenter of Manhattan. "You ready for this, luv?"

Never had a New York landmark been transformed before my eyes more than the 42nd Street building tonight. There had always been something deliciously mysterious about the library when merely walking past it after hours, but knowing we would be ushered into its lavish confines was beyond thrilling. The layers of marble and stone rose regally up, its twisted ivy veil showcased by the glowing spotlights and pops of camera flash. Tall pillar candles in hurricane vases lit the path up the majestic stairs.

I hadn't expected crowds . . . no, make that throngs of people on the sidewalk. I observed the necks craning and eyes straining to catch a glimpse through the tinted windows as we slid to the curb. "Think mermaid, be a mermaid." Mindy's mantra had stuck with me, but I felt more like a fish out of water as our driver stepped lively around to open my door.

Adrian squeezed my hand. "I'm right behind you, Kat."

With my legs demurely pressed together, I swung them out

first, high heels hitting the pavement. Like a regal footman, our driver claimed my hand and hoisted me up. Success.

The chill in the air hit me first, before the night exploded around us. There may have indeed been a carpet, and it could very well have been red, but all I saw were the blinding white flashes of video and still cameras training across me and above me, seeking out their prize as he climbed out of the limo behind me.

"Digger! How does it feel to perform again, after all these years?"

"Tell us how the long-awaited reunion went last night!"

A sea of arms reached out, some wielding cameras, some with microphones, others waving pens hopefully. It was hard to tell the professionals from the amateurs, but it was obvious; the lion's share of people scattered across the glittering sidewalks were fans of Digger Graves.

I waited for Adrian to correct their hopeful questions, to clarify that it had been a one-off gig. That it didn't, as Rick had warned me during that first lonely phone call, spell instant reunion of the band.

"It went off without a hitch," Adrian called out. "It feels great to be back!"

There was an excited murmur from the masses. A dozen flashes caught my face, frozen in time next to their money shot, as his sound bite echoed in my ears.

Our pathway seemed to shrink as the crowd surged forward, and I felt one ankle wobble in my spike heels as I sidestepped to avoid a sign-waver. Luckily, Adrian quickly pressed himself to my opposite side, offering me the crook of his arm and keeping me snug against him as we started to make our way toward the building.

"I fucking love you, Digger!" The sign woman practically blew out my eardrum, screeching the words that were written in glitter paint on her poster board, minus the expletive. She seemed out of place among the Pulitzer Prize–winning authors and MacArthur Geniuses who were filtering by us with less fanfare.

"Are you performing tonight?" Someone hollered, and a buzz of excited laughter followed.

"Goodness, no." Adrian turned and smiled at me. My heels brought us to roughly the same height. "I'm just escorting my lady love on her busman's holiday."

"Who are you wearing?" This time the question was directed at me, and posed by a show-stopping blonde twig of a woman with a dazzling smile. Her own gown was expensively draped over her model's figure, and a microphone boasting the logo of one of the new fashion channels dangled between her long, lacquered nails. "Is it a Chloe? A Stella?"

"It's an Ana," I heard a calm, confident voice say, and I realized it was mine. "She's an up-and coming local designer."

The cameraman accompanying the woman made a whirlybird sign with his finger, and Adrian loosened his grip on me enough so I could give a quick twirl to the left to show off the clever layering and flow of the skirt.

"Fabulous," she raved, "simply fab-u-lous!"

I grinned, thinking of Ana dancing at the nightclub last August to Los Fabulosos Cadillacs in her crazy-high heels.

"Cameron Cook, Digger...from MTV. Can we have a minute of your time?"

"When you start playing music again on your channel, I'm all yours." Adrian allowed a smile in the direction of the news anchor, who didn't appear old enough to have witnessed MTV's original launch.

"When you record new music, we will be sure to air an exclusive." The reporter didn't miss a beat. "Sources say the band is priming for a world tour?"

"Argentina is lovely in spring." Adrian winked, but kept us moving. "And fall."

"So are the rumors true?"

My date paused.

"You're eyeing a three-sixty deal?" Cameron Cook prompted.

Adrian's jaw did a visible shift as he considered his response and obviously thought better of it. "If rumors were true, they'd be fact, mate. And the only fact I'm concerned with right now is being late for this gala if we don't move on. Cheers."

There was more clamoring behind us, but he didn't give another glance to the crowd. "Pay them no mind." He reached for my elbow to steer me, but I pulled away.

"How many people am I going to hear it from before you tell me yourself?" I snapped at him.

"Come on, Kat. You heard me tell Kevin last night we were working on tour routing for the spring."

"I thought you meant a couple of venues around the Northeast. Not . . . not . . . stadiums in South America," I sputtered. "I also heard you tell a five-year-old girl this morning that you weren't going anywhere, anytime soon. You can't have it both ways, Adrian. You just . . . you just can't. I'm sorry."

LIKE CINDERELLA IN REVERSE, I broke from him and marched up the stairs on my own.

"Kat! Katrina!" As nimbly as he had pursued me in Strawberry Fields, Adrian caught up and grabbed ahold of my arm. "Do you really want to do this here? In front of them?"

I turned to look down at the sea of expectant people below us, then back at his pained expression. Years of carefully protected privacy were swirling down the drain, but who was to blame? Who was the one "feeling great" being back? But I had, after all, encouraged him. Because I loved him. Shame flooded my face. "Let's get inside," I managed.

We ascended the steps of the library while Patience and Fortitude, the stone lions I had introduced Adrian to on our first real date, stood guard outside the doors.

Names were murmured, tickets were flashed, and we were ushered into the white-marble entrance of Astor Hall, its cocktail hour already in full swing. The space was just as regal as I remembered from my days of working for the library system, bathed in warm light for the evening's events. Low cocktail tables of white birch awaited, merrily lit by candles and decorated for the season with mossy centerpieces. A trio of classical musicians added their brand of background music to the festivities. But the tension flowing between Adrian and me created a dissonance hard to ignore.

He pulled me under an empty archway, pacing there like a caged beast. "I *can* have it both ways, Kat. You know why? Because I've thought long and hard about this, and I've paid my dues." His cuff link caught the light as he slammed a fist to his chest. "And I'm going to do it the right way, on your schedule, with as little disruption to Abbey's life as possible. You've got to trust me on this."

"I do, but . . ."

"I know it's a crazy ride. But this time around, *I'm* calling the shots." He placed his hands on my shoulders. "I'm controlling the roller coaster. Who gets a ride, and who gets off. It's gonna go at my pace, all right?"

"Once it picks up speed, it's going to be hard to stop," I whispered. "Even if you want to."

Adrian dipped his head down, searching out my eyes. "Okay. So are we going to close our eyes and fight it the whole way? Or are we going to let go and enjoy the thrill of it?"

I placed my hands on his where they rested on my shoulders. He must not have seen an answer he liked in my eyes, because he broke away before I could speak. "I need a drink," he muttered. "Do you want one?"

I bit my lip, shaking my head. I could barely handle the carousel ride in Central Park. Could I sign myself on for this? Or Abbey?

I stood and watched couple after well-dressed couple glide by me. Young ones, old ones. Lovers, friends, family. I thought about how I'd bandied about Corroded Corpse lyrics in conversation with my brother earlier. The song had been the aptly named "Trust in Me," and another verse came to mind.

Let's live for today
Think of the demons we'll slay
Plenty of stories for when we're old and gray

Could I throw all the worries and "what ifs" to the wind? Adrian and I had gotten this far without a plan, after all.

"I don't want to fight," I told him when he returned. "But I need to understand. What's a three-sixty deal?"

Adrian downed his first drink of the night and drummed his fingers on the rough-hewn table in front of us. "That's nothing. Totally unconfirmed."

"It's something," I said. "You were right next to me, and now you are a million miles away at the mere mention of it."

A gusty sigh escaped, causing the decorative votive in front of him to flicker. "Just considering the source of the rumor, that's all."

"Something tells me a three-sixty is not even close to 398.2 on the Dewey Decimal number line." My lame library joke brought a soft smile to Adrian's face.

"Say this is your band, your star power." Reaching across the cocktail table, he centered the small, lit candle. "Then you've got all your music-related projects. Your studio recordings "—he set down his whiskey glass at the midnight position—"your live shows"—my evening bag was plunked down at six o'clock—"and your merchandise, your TV ads, your movie soundtracks . . ."

He systematically emptied his pockets of his wallet, loose

change, and his ever-present guitar picks, assigning a place around the table to each item in turn, each representing a piece of the pie. "And depending on which devil you make your deal with, whether it's the record label or the promoter"—he counted them off on his thumb and forefinger—"they take the rights to it all. And round and round it goes, until your bright star burns out."

To emphasize his point, he licked his thumb and pinched out the flame. "The end." Unflinching, he took back custody of his whiskey glass and drained its dregs.

Talk about your grim fairy tales, I thought. "That's crazy."

"That's the new music model," came a voice from behind us. Rick picked up one of Adrian's picks, inspected its gauge, and pocketed it. "But you forgot a piece."

"Ah, yes. The money grab. The band gets a cool five million—"

"Ten," Rick corrected. He handed Adrian back his wallet. "Up front."

"If we sell our soul to them for the next ten years."

"No, five."

Adrian swept the rest of the sundry items back into his hand. "Someone's been negotiating."

"Someone's been exploring the options." Rick shook up the ice in his glass and consulted it, as if the cubes might take on a shape and tell his fortune, like tea leaves.

"How about you take the night off, Magellan. No brave new world to discover here."

Rick frowned slightly. "Wasn't planning on even bringing it up, mate. Until I heard you speak of it."

"Really." The word fell flat from Adrian's lips. Not so much a question but a testing statement. "You didn't leak it to the music press, then?"

"Sam." Rick said instantly. "I warned you not to even tell him, Dig."

Adrian slowly shook his head. "And I didn't."

I placed a hand on my date's arm, which seemed to bring him back to his surroundings.

"Enough, no matter." He glanced around. "Are your in-laws here tonight?"

"Out of the country. Hence the extra seats at this little slice of literary heaven. Kat," Rick leaned to kiss my cheek. "You're a vision."

"Thank you. For both the compliment, and the tickets."

After poring over all those old band pictures, I had to jolt myself back into reality as I stared up at this twenty-first-century version of Riff Rotten. Just a hint of stubble shadowed his scalp, where long, ebony locks once flowed. His features were classic Mediterranean, from heavy brow to strong nose, and even more striking without the mane of hair to hide behind. Facial hair was trimmed to a minimum, neatly surrounding his sculpted jaw and meeting in a dark point under a full bottom lip. One detail remained the same. His onyx eyes burned with the same hungry intensity.

"Well now," Adrian conceded, flicking Rick's starched collar. "Aren't you the dog's dinner?"

Like its guitarist, the band's customarily shirtless and screaming front man was a different animal when attired in formalwear. Adrian may've held the title for Most Deliberately Rugged Tuxedo-Clad Male, but Rick? He wore a tuxedo like it was his job and calling. Like he was the James Bond of heavy metal.

"Either way you slice it," Rick deadpanned.

"Slumming it solo tonight?" Adrian asked his best mate. There had been women to the left and right of the singer backstage the night before.

He just gave a noncommittal shrug. "Guess I'm a free agent now. What are you two lovers drinking tonight?"

Servers had been mingling with flutes of champagne on

trays, but I wasn't in the mood for the bubble and fizz. "I feel something classic calling, standing between you debonair gents. How about a martini? Dry and dirty."

Rick's brow shot up, then he nodded his approval.

"Basil Hayden. On the rocks." Adrian handed Rick his empty glass.

"Ah, behaving yourself. Noted."

Adrian turned to me, once Rick ambled toward the bar. "Dry and dirty, eh? 'Tis a pity we've given up showering together, luv. However will I get you wet . . . and clean?"

A slow smile spread across my face, but desire moved like a wildfire across the desert plains within me. "You'll just have to get creative, I guess."

Fingers ghosted the tiny pleats of material swathing my waist as Adrian claimed it. His touch was warm and welcoming. "First order of business when we get home," he said. "After I steal you away from the intellectually chic this evening."

It seemed I had successfully taken his mind off music business for now. But in my own mind, we still had some unfinished business of our own. The argument felt small and petty now, hanging high above our heads in the hallowed hall.

THREADING my bare arm through his jacket-clad one, I snuggled up against him and we turned to people watch. Well-dressed socialites and philanthropists mixed and mingled, and it was fun to take in their clothing styles and try to decide whether they were famous or not. I thought I spotted Candice Bergen and Barbara Walters. Adrian pointed out an elegant woman and claimed she was a Jordanian princess. "I've heard she's a big patron of the arts."

"What do you think people are saying about us?" I joked, squeezing tighter.

"Hmmm . . . 'There's the prettiest librarian in the room, whatever does she see in that ruffian?'"

Adrian was back to trilling each *r* like a dog wrestling with a chew toy, and he nuzzled his final word against my temple.

"Oh, please!" I whipped to face him, and tested out the kissable factor of my lipstick. "You're my diamond in the rough."

"Pardon me . . . I couldn't help but overhear you say she was a librarian." A slim gentleman approached, his business card extending from between two fingers. "*Town & Country* magazine. We're running a feature on the gala next week. I'd be interested to hear your thoughts on the importance of tonight's benefit, from a librarian's perspective."

"Oh goodness," I said hastily. "I haven't worked for the library in several years, I don't know if I— you see . . ."

"Once a librarian, always a librarian." Adrian stroked my arm fondly, and gave the man a winning smile. "I fell in love with her in a library."

"Full circle," the man murmured, taking notes in his head. "I'm afraid I must hurry to catch the library president before dinner begins, but please do call me this week. My cell and office numbers are on the card. I'd love to include both of you in the article." With a pleased smile, he rushed off.

"Adrian!" I practically belted him with the brass knuckles of my evening bag. "Don't go telling tales out of school."

"What? I did fall for you that day." He grinned. "And each day after."

"You had beer goggles that day."

"That's tosh! I was smitten . . . even after I had sobered up. And it was Jack Daniels, for the record." Adrian rocked back on his heels. "I'm surprised you let me within fifty feet of those children."

"Well, let's not share *that* story with the press, okay?" Call it a lapse in judgment or a leap of faith, but I had believed in Adrian Graves and the magic of his music that day, and he had not disappointed. "I'm sure they will run wild at the mere notion of the 'librarian and rock star' stereotype."

"Speaking of that day, Ms. Lew-*is* . . . if you would be so good as to excuse me?"

"Going for a slash?" I couldn't resist teasing Adrian with the British slang he'd used upon our first meeting, causing him to erupt in a full-on belly laugh.

"Stop, please! Yes, before I burst."

I gave his arm a push. "Go, you goof." He gave a mock bow in thanks as he backed away, and then hurried off in the direction of the restrooms. Chuckling, I checked my phone. Luke had texted earlier, reporting that all was fine with Abbey, but I hadn't had a chance to respond. I quickly thumbed back: *Kiss her good night for me. You should see this place—unreal!*

I glanced around, trying to decide if I could do any of the scenery justice by snapping a photo. My pro-photographer brother-in-law adored taking pictures of New York landmarks, and I was sure he would appreciate an exclusive peek, even through my not-so-very-artistic eye. I moved to snap a stealth photo of an elaborate pyre-like structure of birch logs that flanked a tall candelabrum.

"Ah, there she is!"

Turning, I found two gentlemen, one older and distinguished, the other younger and obviously drunk as he opened his arms wide and began spouting poetry in my general direction. *"Strutting 'cross the heavenly blue, piercing backs of stars in her . . .* what kind of shoes are you wearing, lass?"

"Um . . . I don't know," I admitted. My shoes had appeared with my dress. The whole ensemble couldn't have come together any more magically and mysteriously, even if woodland creatures themselves had delivered each item through the window, transforming me into their Central Park Cinderella.

"She doesn't know!" The younger man's accent was melodically Irish, even when doused with drink. "A woman who doesn't know her own brand of shoe? How utterly rare and refreshing!"

"If I told you I found them in my boyfriend's closet, would you believe me?"

This delighted him. He turned to the older man. "I think I love her. Can I love her?"

"Easy, Roddy." Under curly locks of salt and pepper hair, the Irishman's companion directed a wink my way. "There's a formidable contender already composing poetry about her."

"Bugger, shit, and piss! You've broken my heart, lassie."

The Irishman grabbed my hand to kiss it, before turning on his heel and calling after another women, "*Strutting 'cross the heavenly blue, piercing backs of stars in her . . .*"

"Wait . . . poetry . . . that wasn't Roddy—?"

"Finnegan? Yes."

"The poet laureate?"

"The same. Don't worry. Dinner will sober him up and he'll be composing better prose by night's end. One of his esteemed colleagues, who's up for one of the creative medals of achievement tonight, challenged him to compose a Horatian ode in the style of an epinician, with a fetish thrown in for good measure. Or perhaps I should say, good *meter*."

We both chuckled at his joke. Suddenly remembering social grace, I stuck out my hand. "Hi, I'm Katrina Lewis."

"I know. I had to come over to meet you. I'm Alexander Floyd. And you're currently every rock journalist's wet dream."

∾

"I AM?" I asked, astonished. "I mean, eww, really?"

Alexander Floyd—it was hard not to automatically attach his last name to his first name, since I had always seen it that way, in every byline I had encountered—smiled.

"Sorry, that was a crude way of saying you broke not only

the one story every music writer hopes to in a lifetime, but then you went and blew our minds by breaking another. Finding both Digger Graves and Riff Rotten, *and* getting them to speak to each other after fifteen years of stubborn silence?" He just shook his head in awe.

"It wasn't so hard," I said. "I just went and looked for them in the least likely of places." My own words prompted me to crane my neck, on the lookout for my impeccably dressed, rough-and-tumble rocker to come ambling through one of the archways within the marbled foyer of the library.

"So I heard." His smirk was a friendly one.

"Speaking of which, is that why you're here tonight?"

"Me? No." He shook the ice in his glass and laughed. "I don't just write for the rock rags, Katrina. I came to watch all the muckety-mucks being honored with major literary awards. Seeing the guys here . . . just a happy coincidence."

"When was the last time you saw them? I mean, besides last night. That was a nice write-up in the *Muse*, by the way."

"Thanks. The last time I saw them? Well, the last time I saw Digger was . . ." He trailed off, pushing the curls off his forehead to reveal a shiny, jagged scar.

"You . . . oh my God, you were there the night of his arrest?"

It had taken a lot for Adrian to share the details of that painful memory with me. Of Simone, crying in the all-night diner as the paparazzi descended. And his feelings of anger, of helplessness, and finally, his lashing out.

"I was in the midst of writing their biography. When a photographer friend tipped me off to his whereabouts, I couldn't resist checking it out." He gave a grim smile at my expression. "Not proud to have contributed to the melee. We were all a bit crazy in the eighties, I suppose."

"But you weren't breaking plates over people's heads," I pointed out.

"True," he admitted with a laugh. "It never changed how I

felt about the band, though. Their music, well . . . it awakened something in me, long ago. I've never been religious so I have no clue what's it's like to feel born again, but the fervor, the zeal? I get it. So thank you. On behalf of Corpse fans everywhere."

"I'm . . . I'm not so sure I did the right thing," I stammered. "What if— What if it all blows up again?" There were words I couldn't even voice, not to this almost-stranger, not to my close friends, and not even to myself. *What if I lose him?*

"People change. Take me: older, wiser . . . a little grayer." He chuckled. "We move on. Grow up. Grow out of things. There might still be that tiny spark in there," he clutched a fist to the middle of his chest. "That fervor, that zeal. It never dies. But so many things happen to us, to change us, in the meantime. You're never going to look at it, or act on it, in exactly the same way. So why not embrace it again, and come what may?"

The truth of what he said hit me. We all live with our scars, whether hidden under our shirts or curls, or etched deep into our hearts and minds. We may share them; they're a part of who we are. But moving past them? That's the real badge of honor. Adrian and I had already been through so much, together and apart. There was no way not to embrace the unknown. Whatever was to be, with the band or our future, we were strong enough to face it together.

"I won't keep you. Enjoy the evening, Katrina." He pressed his palm warmly against mine. Then— his voice suddenly turning shy and unsure, like a teen come to call at his date's front door—he stammered, "Do you think I could . . . would it be okay if I stopped by your table after dinner to visit you?"

The "you" he was implying was a collective one, his query an unspoken request that was light years more respectful than those reporters outside, flinging their questions in our faces. And, like the recent words of Roddy Finnegan, utterly rare and refreshing. Ironically, I kept thinking of all the questions I could be asking him. Alexander Floyd was an oracle, the leading authority on the band, outside of the band itself. And yet he was considering me a gatekeeper.

"I think that would be just fine." We smiled and slipped past each other.

I reached Adrian just as trumpeters heralded the start of dinner, and hundreds of highbrow guests began to herd themselves like cattle into the next room.

"Ah, there you are." Adrian reached for my hand. "I thought perhaps Rick absconded with you, and our drinks, onto a slow boat bound for China."

"He's still not back yet?"

I caught sight of Rick by the bar, just as a strikingly glamorous woman sidled up to him. Her dress poured over her as if it were molten lava, blue-black in its color, like the deepest center of a flame. And like moths in their well-dressed woolens, every man within a ten-foot radius was drawn to her. Legs that had no intention of quitting, stacked on expensive looking stilettos, peeked through the side-slit in her skirt as she leaned to commune with Rick's ear. She tilted her complicated, highlighted blonde updo toward him in consultation.

Rick's face remained impassive as he listened to whatever she was dictating. Then a frown and a shake of his head sent her strutting off importantly in the other direction. I swear I saw the gala's ice sculpture shiver as she passed it.

Adrian stiffened at my side. The grip on my hand was so tight, his Shakespeare ring I wore bit into my fingers. I imagined its scrolling design leaving an imprint of its words on my skin: WE KNOW WHAT WE ARE.

"Isabelle." The name blew from his lips like a curse.

"Who is she?" I asked.

"She's a lot of things," he said slowly. "But mostly, she was a bad habit."

~

"Remember when I told you Wren hired me a personal assistant?"

I nodded, remembering exactly what he had said: basically, someone to help him shoot up so he wouldn't die. My imagination had instantly assigned some nameless, faceless "bad guy," a shady shadow in Adrian's life. Not female. And certainly not one who looked like she had just stepped off one of the sports car posters keeping all the rockers company on my brother's teenage fantasy wall. "Her?"

Adrian's chin dropped, then jutted in the affirmative. "He had her doing our U.S. publicity, too, so I suppose Isabelle had a vested interest in keeping me alive."

Rick approached us with drinks in hand, threading through the steady current of gala guests flooding toward the South-North Gallery.

"Egotistic, self-serving—she even makes a big league control freak like Rick look like a rookie."

"Do you think he's . . . *with* her? Now?"

Their interchange had looked . . . intimate, to say the least. Perhaps she was the source of the industry rumors. Perhaps Rick had been an unwitting supplier of gossip . . . maybe he talked in his sleep.

"Never." Adrian practically spat. "She was Simone's best friend. I trust that even he has limits."

I had no time to digest that.

"Here we are then." Rick held two squat whiskey glasses in one strong hand, and my martini in the other. "Dry and dirty, just how the lady likes it. And weak and watered down, for the gentleman. I believe that bombastic blast of the trumpet means dinner is to be served."

"You invited Isabelle?" Adrian was halfway through his drink by the time we neared the Celeste Bartos Forum.

"I didn't have to. She's on the board of Simone's charity foundation."

Adrian shot daggers across the doorway. "And I suppose she is sitting at our table, too?"

"She chairs various other nonprofit efforts for my in-laws." Rick explained.

In other words, yes.

Adrian looked like he wanted to pull the chair right out from under the woman as she settled at a table in the corner.

"Ten ruddy years on this island, I've managed to avoid her. Fifteen years since I purged her from my life, and tonight? Of all nights?" His eyes sparked their blue embers. "And why are you pledging allegiance to her, when you should be burning the flag in protest?"

"Any more questions?" Rick wisecracked.

"No. I now have no doubts as to who tipped off the press."

"And I had no idea she'd have such an effect on you." Rick said blithely.

"She doesn't. She *reminds* me. Of what a monster I was." Adrian jammed his hands into his pockets. "I need a moment. Some air. A smoke."

"Adrian . . ." I began, but my lover had already turned, his dress shoes echoing down the polished corridor.

"Oh, for fuck's sake," Rick sputtered. "There he goes again, from hero to victim. Isn't that what I told you, Kat? Everything's so black-and-white with him. Why can't he just muck about in the gray matter for a while?"

"*Strutting 'cross the heavenly blue!*" Roddy was back, but he had found a new muse, apparently. Isabelle. We witnessed him, intervening her approach. "*Piercing backs of stars in her . . .* are those Jimmy Choos you're wearing, by any chance?"

Rick's companion may have had a face like an angel, but her mouth was like the Fresh Kills landfill.

"Fuck off, Finnegan." Her accent was brusque and full of all five boroughs. "I don't have time for your shit." Laughing, the poet laureate stumbled away just as smoothly as he had sidled up to her. "Riff! I've been looking for you *for ages*."

The stare she fixed on me as she finished her sentence gave me the feeling she didn't just mean tonight, and that she resented the hell out of me for beating her to it.

Rick may have spent the last two decades hiding out in Hawaii, but he hadn't forgotten his manners. "Katrina Lewis, Isabelle Garmin . . . Iz, this is Kat."

I watched her with a mix of fascination and trepidation. The big flat rocks at the lake came to mind, the ones Kev and I would lift as children, never knowing what we would find under them. The treasure trove of glittering beetles and fat, squirming grubs would send us running, flinging the rocks back down in delighted horror.

"Yes," she said flatly. "I figured."

Before I had a chance to comment, a petite woman crossed our path. Her sleek chignon and searching look instantly alerted me to press. It was getting easier to tell as the night wore on.

"Maya Patel, Mr. Rotten. *Vogue* magazine. May I ask who you're wearing tonight?"

"Burberry." The brand trickled off his tongue, and the writer gave an approving nod. "I thought so. The cut, the virgin wool . . ."

"It's the *only* virgin he wears these days." Isabelle claimed Rick's arm.

"Hello, Isabelle . . . in Versace?" Maya asked, and I thought I caught a hint of predictability in her voice.

"Always." She clung to Rick's arm and smiled for cameras that weren't there.

"This is pretty." The reporter gestured at my dress. "Which house is it from?"

I knew she meant fashion house, but I almost laughed,

picturing their faces if I said it was from the house of Digger Graves. "A friend made it for me."

"Homemade?" Isabelle's expertly made up eyes surveyed me with a cool glance, making me feel as if I were the one living under the rock. Writhing and grubby.

"Excuse me." A woman in stunning attire of gold and black touched my arm. "My husband and I saw you earlier, and I just had to come over to say how exquisite you look." She beamed and shook her head, gazing at my silhouette. "Easily the most interesting gown in the room, don't you agree, ladies?"

I noticed everyone standing a bit taller in her presence. Maya nodded enthusiastically. Isabelle gave the feminine equivalent to my ex-boyfriend Grant's famous just-eaten-a-bug look.

"Thank you." I smiled at the kind woman. "I like yours, too," I added, as she floated away with a nod to everyone else.

"You *do* know who that was, right?" Maya asked.

"Jesus Christ," Isabelle huffed, glancing at her diamond-encrusted watch. Clearly she was done with amateur hour.

"I'll give you a hint," Maya turned back to me, eyes sparkling. "Her husband's name is Oscar and he's a bit of a celebrity."

The only somewhat famous Oscars I was familiar with were the little gold statues, the puppet on Sesame Street, and Oscar de la Renta. And since Isabelle appeared to be the only Grouch in the room . . .

Rick laughed at my wide-eyed expression as if he had been waiting for it. "She and her husband are co-chairs of tonight's event. That was quite a compliment."

"Are you kidding? That was like a love letter in a bottle." Maya enthused. "I'd love to see more of your friend's work. Could I call her?"

"Sure," I said, taking the pad and pen she handed me, and jotting down Adrian's home number. "Wednesday afternoons are best." I selfishly hoped I was at his house when Ana picked up the phone and realized it was *Vogue* on the line.

Isabelle wasted no time grabbing the spotlight after the reporter bid us goodnight. "So where's your boyfriend? Getting high in the bathroom?"

"Ah, Iz." Rick sighed. "Such a joy. Really. It's great to be back."

Rick's comment echoed Adrian's earlier quip to the reporters, and bounced off the thin walls of my defenses. His knowing eyes rested on me, waiting for some kind of reaction.

"Adrian's been clean for over ten years."

"Damn," she pouted. "I liked him dirty. Did you know shooting heroin gives a guy a boner as stiff as a fucking lead pipe? I hope for your sake he's at least using Viagra."

"Isabelle. Enough." Rick grunted.

"Ah, look. It's Damien from *The Examiner*. Kisses, Damien darling!"

"She's the monster. Not Adrian," I choked from under my rage and tears, as she strutted off to air kiss.

"You think that's bad? Wait until you hear what she'll say behind your back. You're going to have to grow a thicker skin in this business, you know. If you want to be with him."

"Oh?" I reeled to face him. "Is there a playbook for us gals that I should be following? Did Simone have one?"

A muscle in Rick's cheek twitched. "You know what they call gals like you, right? The ones we musicians love but leave behind, time after time? *Road widows.* Are you ready for that, Kat? All over again?"

"How dare you." My words were barely above a whisper.

"I'm saying that out of the utmost respect, sweetheart. Playtime is over. You've got to be the strong one. You can't be a bottomless pit of need. Or you will lose him."

"Oh, and then you'll win, right? Because misery loves company, and you will have him right back where you want him." I thought back to all the photos, all the stories. The empty stardom that had shot a crater of unhappiness through the man I loved. It wasn't going to happen again, not if I could help it. "You can't stand the thought of being the Have Not in this round, can you?"

He needed to back the fuck down, because I wasn't.

"Touché, darling. That's a start." The arch of his smile was devilishly handsome. "It's about time someone stuck up for him."

"You're amused?"

"No, just halfway to drunk." He flashed open his fancy tux jacket, and strapped against its smart vest was a lethal-looking flask. "I hate these bloody social events."

I couldn't help myself. The sob that had been threatening to break free all evening came out as a laugh. I couldn't help myself—I liked Riff Rotten.

"SHALL WE?" Rick offered up his arm. "I can't just leave you here, like a damsel in distress." I hesitated, glancing down the empty hallway behind us. "Or I guess you'd rather wait for your white knight?"

I gave him a smile and shook my head. I was done waiting, and I didn't need to be rescued. Gathering the bottom of my dress in my hands, I began to hurry down the long gallery, my heels like firecrackers on the marble.

"Hey, where's the fire?" Adrian caught me as I skittered around the polished corner and almost crashed smack into him.

"Should we just forget this? Get out of here and go on home?"

Adrian looked a bit defeated. "I'm afraid I don't have any more surprises waiting for you back home, Kat. Just me."

"That's all I need," I insisted. "All I've ever needed."

I kissed him as if I could take away every unpleasant memory, and he responded as if I was all the happiness he knew.

"Remember what you said to me in the limo? About conquering the world with me on your arm, and by your side?" I searched his eyes until I saw something familiar in them. "I'm right here. I'm not going anywhere," I said quietly.

Adrian's handsome features softened, and the brittle edge of his voice was soft and supple once more. "I love you. For always, Kat. And I want to stay."

"So let's rock this busman's holiday."

Together, we entered the vast space that had been transformed into a lush winter setting for the heady and elegant evening. A rustic, winter forest of bare, white birch trees delicately lined the perimeter of the room, appearing to fade off into the distance. Under the grand iron skylight, chandeliers adorned with bark and branches shimmered, paired with crystals and disco balls for a wintery glimmer. Each table was set softly aglow with candles in birch log holders, tucked around centerpieces of moss and nests, pears and white roses. To my delight, programs made to look like old leather-bound books topped each place setting.

Silent waiters made their rounds with sumptuous courses: smoked salmon Napoleon, chicken scaloppine with braised fennel and fava beans, morels and asparagus. Coffee followed, as did warm brownie pudding paired with vanilla bean ice cream. Thankfully, Isabelle didn't sit still for more than a bite of each; she was up and schmoozing, making the rounds. But every so often, I'd catch her eyeing our trio. Making it known she was the type of woman who got what she wanted, and it was clear she wanted back into the inner sanctum. Only time would tell, I supposed. That was up to the real gatekeepers, who sat on either side of me.

Tributes were made at the microphone, and the library's president thanked the four hundred attendees, as over one and a half million dollars had been raised for the library's book fund by the event. Then, as each Library Lions medal was presented, the honorees held court, each reflecting on how they'd used the resources at the library during the course of their achievements.

It was amusing to watch the two rockers, reclining easily in their Chiavari chairs. They looked dashing and a little dangerous, clapping politely and conferring every now and again behind me, with a tilt of Adrian's shaggy head toward Rick's neatly shaven one.

But neither of them were as stunned as I was when they were called up to present a medal of achievement to one Mister Alexander Floyd.

"Two questions for you lads." Alexander stood at my chair, his new medal gleaming from the bottom of its wide, red ribbon.

"Where were you during our press conference before the Garden gig, yeah?" Rick wanted to know. "You snooze, you lose, Alex, dear boy."

A round of laughter and groans of "oh, come on" from the award-winning journalist commenced.

"Two. Two and only two." Rick slung an arm across Adrian's shoulders and dialed up an exaggerated stony stare. "Go for it," he commanded.

Adrian gave his best mate a jostling with his elbow, jutting his chin for the cameras that had trailed after Alexander. "Shoot."

The pair mugged adorably for the cameras, just like the days of old. Together, they radiated a sensual energy that could only come from two dynamic talents who had played off of each other's strengths and weaknesses for years. The potency had strengthened during their estrangement. If performing was akin to an orgasmic experience for Adrian, I could only imagine that the band's reunion was like the best make-up sex ever.

"Digger, what were Riff's last words to you, back in '88?"

"I believe they were"—Adrian smirked, and in his best imitation of Rick's slightly more cultivated tone—"'See you in hell, me old China.'"

"And Riff? Digger's first words to you last month?"

Rick suppressed a laugh, and captured Adrian's murmur spot-on. "'Hell's a right bit chilly, ain't it? Seems to 'ave frozen over.' Wasn't that it, mate?" He pulled back to look fondly upon his blood brother.

Alexander furiously scribbled in his notepad, shaking his head and grinning at this rare exclusive he was getting. "And when do you plan on growing that glorious hair back?"

It was as if Rick hadn't heard the question, the way he turned back to the conversation being held at the table with a distracted smile. Then again, it had been Alexander's third question, and Rick had only agreed to two.

"Alex, have you met Kat yet?" Adrian slid an arm around my waist and kissed my cheek.

"Has he met me yet?" I joked. "I'm the one who invited him over."

"Inviting the paparazzi to our table?" Adrian sputtered in mock horror. "That's unheard of!"

"Revolutionary," Alexander agreed. "Perhaps I should write an article about *you* someday, my dear."

Déjà vu sliced through me like a double-edged sword. Adrian had once, during a moment of raw frustration, expressed his wish that someone would write a book about me, because he just couldn't crack me.

"Did Digger put you up to that?" I glanced at my lover now, but his gaze had locked on me first, a smile playing on his lips. He'd done one better. He'd written a song about me.

No smoke and mirrors, no saints here,
Only saviors, survivors, no fear
Catch a glimpse of the future
Emerald eyes hold it clear . . .

He now knew me better than anyone, I was sure of that.

"Are you kidding?" Alexander laughed. "He barely puts up with me, period. Who needs to remember the Alamo when we've got the Applejack Diner?"

Adrian winced. "Sorry about that Blue Plate Special to your bonce, mate."

"You can make it up to me now, with a drink at the bar. And a chat."

"Go," I said, when Adrian turned to me. This night really wasn't just about me, and I was perfectly fine with that.

"Only if he gives this exclusive the headline 'Life After Death' . . . there is more to my life"—he smiled and corrected himself—"to *our* life, than Corroded Corpse, after all."

"You're very different than his prior conquests, you know."

Dinner was winding down, but Riff Rotten was just winding up. He allowed the waiters to swoop in with their crumb brushes, whisking away plates and glasses until only his silver flask of single malt Scotch remained. "Robyn was about as shallow as a child's paddling pool," he continued, unprompted. "You are deeper than that."

"Yes, we've already established that. I am a bottomless pit of need."

"No." Rick did the drunk sway, elbows on the table, and frowned like he was disagreeing with both himself and me.

"That was just me being a jealous bastard. You're even deeper than that. You're his dream girl."

"And Isabelle?"

Rick waved a hand to dismiss the thought. "She's soulless. This business sucked her dry."

"Then why are you aligning yourself with her? Out of loyalty to Simone?"

"Can we change the subject, please?" He stared stonily into his glass; his expression the perfect accompaniment to the phrase "all clammed up."

It reminded me of the question I wanted to ask him.

"Care to tell me how this came into Abbey's possession?"

I slid the shell across the table.

Rick rested a long, elegant finger on its ridged hump. He didn't speak for a moment. "I gave it to her as *makana aloha*." The Hawaiian words sounded more magical when siphoned through his British accent. "A gift of love."

"You know what it is, don't you?"

Rick smiled. "Why don't you tell me, Miss Marple?" He slid it smoothly back across to me, leaned back, and folded his arms across his chest. "We are on your turf, after all."

Of course the library sleuth in me had been curious, and I'd had a chance to run a quick search on it—not within the city's flagship temple of learning, but online, back at Adrian's. "It's a Langford's Pecten. Otherwise known as the rare sunrise shell. Although, this one's color makes it a moonrise shell, hence an even rarer specimen."

"Bravo," Rick said, barely above a whisper, raising his eyes toward the gently curved glass ceiling to avoid meeting mine.

"They're worth about a hundred dollars a pop." I carefully set it back in front of him. "Why would you give one to a five-year-old?"

"It's worthless to me." Rick once again pushed it away. "I lost its mate, years ago." I heard his words, but it was the haunted look in his eyes that I truly understood. "You see . . . it's rare to find a single moonrise shell." He placed it in my hand, bumpy side down. "But to find a natural matched pair, well . . . that happens once in a lifetime."

I let its cool weight rest against my open palm, and tried to imagine its other half.

"Simone was crazy about them. She'd comb the beach for hours at dawn, just hoping to catch a glimpse of that flicker of color, lying in the sand. She even enlisted our boys—Paul, Jonah, Ari—her faithful army, in her quest." A pained laugh broke through his memory. "I thought she had completely lost the plot . . . you know?" He spun his finger at the side of his head. "Gone crazy. I couldn't see the point of her wanting one so desperately. Until it dawned on me, she needed one."

Rick's dark eyes pleaded understanding. He didn't want to voice it, and I didn't make him. In my research, I'd learned that the shells represented hope, strength, and protection.

"So who finally found this one?" I asked quietly.

Rick smirked. "Digger always said I wouldn't know a good thing even if it jumped up and bit me on the arse. I stepped on it. Blasted thing nearly sliced my toe off."

He gently traced the shell's ruffled edge where it was nestled in my hand. From afar, it must've looked like he was reading my palm. And perhaps, in a way, he was. Fortune-telling through his own eyes and experiences.

"See where it's jagged here? It must've weathered some rough surf. But the wings are its most delicate part, and they are intact. There was ligament at one time, hinging the two sides when we found it. Simone both celebrated and mourned it; joined at the hip like us, she said. But it was empty inside." *Also like us*, the sad dwindle in his voice implied.

I thought back to Adrian's story of the night he was arrested; of Simone confiding that she'd finally decided to leave Rick, for good. That obviously hadn't happened. Death had parted them first.

"No two sides are the same, you know," he continued in that quiet murmur. His voice had a velvet quality to it, and a pitch indicative of the many ranges he could reach while singing. "The top half, brighter. And the bottom half, smoother. Perfectly paired, but quite different."

We both glanced toward the bar. Adrian was in deep discussion with Alexander, good-naturedly wagging a finger to prove a point. The reporter was gazing with rapt attention, yet his anticipation was palpable, ready to interrupt at any moment but respectfully refraining. Until Adrian paused to take a sip of his whiskey, and Alexander launched into his litany. Adrian glanced my way, catching my eye and winking.

"Like I said before. Once in a lifetime."

"Twice, if you're lucky," I insisted. The grim twist of Rick's lips dimpled his cheek and mocked my optimism. He moved a hand under mine, his strong thumb pushing my fingers closed over my palm and his gift.

"Enjoy it." His face was once again impassive. I carefully deposited the shell back into my evening bag. His *makana aloha* may have been intended for Abbey, but the message of peace he offered seemed to be directed straight at me.

"Is that our limo waiting?" I nodded toward the long black stretch at the curb as we began our descent down the regal stairs.

"I believe it is. Perfect timing, no?" Adrian asked, and I almost expected a clock somewhere to begin chiming midnight.

"Well, let's use it, before it turns back into a pumpkin," I joked.

"Wait, wait." His eyes surveyed the steps. "Yes, it was exactly here." He pulled me down to sit next to him on a stone-cold step. "This is where I found Patience." He turned to the stone lion at our right and tipped an imaginary hat. "'Ello, guv'nor."

"And this is where I'd so hoped I'd find you," I whispered, snuggling close to kiss him.

"*Easy, Tiger . . .*" he sang the words, just as he had during the concert the night before, but this time the lyrics were for my ears only, from the first to the last, as he wound his tuxedo jacket around my bare shoulders and held me close.

"Adrian Graves," I admonished, "did you go and write me a heavy metal love song?"

"Well now, maybe I did."

"I thought if love was going to appear in your music, it had to be doomed, damned, or deadly," I teased, quoting words he used in the past. He sat back to look at me, and the raise of his brow indicated he wasn't the only one who remembered a surprising number of details.

"I've learned since that love runs much deeper than that." His arm tightened around my waist, pulling me even closer. "Deeper than dreams," he murmured against the shell of my ear. "And if I've made even one of your dreams come true tonight, then I am a better man for it."

His gaze caught mine and I felt the world stop for a moment. All the attention and fuss during the day had been fun and surreal. But it made no difference whether we were standing side stage at the Garden right before showtime, by the lake watching Abbey chase the seagulls, or dressed to the nines in the freezing cold while a gala raged on behind us. Side by side, in it together.

There was no place else my head, my heart, and my body wanted to be.

"Are you ready to go home?"

Now I was certain; bells were ringing somewhere. Maybe

back in Adrian's spacious Manhattan apartment, or up at my cozy house in Lauder Lake, where it took three minutes for the motley menagerie of clocks to welcome in the midnight hour. Home was anywhere we were, whether it was somewhere out on tour, or right here on Fifth Avenue. And even if the road separated us for a while, we'd be home . . . because home was love, as well.

Adrian stood, and then slowly backed down a couple of steps, his gaze never leaving me. Despite the chilly November temperature, he began to roll up his shirtsleeves.

"What are you—"

As if he were about to be knighted, my prince knelt on one step in front of me. He extended his bare forearm, and there, wound between the tattooed cat paws, were words written in Abbey's childish scrawl:

Mommy, will you marry Adrian Graves please?

Yet another person he had enlisted to help pull off this magical evening, right under my nose.

He had, literally, had something up his sleeve the whole time. And he had managed to keep it from me all day, under wraps . . . and even in the shower.

My mouth dropped open. With a smile, Adrian handed me a Sharpie marker from his back pocket and put a finger to my lips. As a former librarian, I knew all about silence, and how it could sometimes be, for better and for worse, even louder than love.

Taking his left hand in mine, I inked *Y E S !* across his four knuckles.

Adrian gave a rebel yell and swooped me into his arms. The limo door burst open, and there was Abbey, racing up to join in our embrace.

"Well?" Luke and Kimon climbed out of the limo next, followed by Liz and Kev.

"What'd she say?" My brother hollered up the steps between cupped hands.

Grinning, Adrian gave a strong fist pump into the air triumphantly, as Abbey hugged our legs. There were cheers and claps from not only my family below, but from the bystanders and gala guests who had gathered nearby to watch.

Rick stood with his arms crossed, a slight smile playing across his handsome face and softening his chiseled jaw. Was it a smile of consent, or of defeat? I didn't know him well enough to read him just yet.

Isabelle approached him from behind. She tugged at his shoulder with one hand, while impatiently hailing her waiting Town Car with the other, but he didn't react.

"Mommy, I think Dad's winking at us!" Abbey gasped.

I gazed far above our heads, up at the clear view of stars. I imagined Pete up there with the brightest of them. *You had a journalist propose to you in a rock club.* He'd chuckle over the irony. *Only fitting to have a rock star propose to you at a library.*

Adrian nestled something solid over my ring finger. "Chatoyant," he said of the brilliant green stone in its antique, diamond-surrounded setting. "A cat's eye emerald, for my Kat." Kissing my knuckle, he added, "For always."

I wanted Abbey to grow up with Adrian in her life. And I wanted to grow old with him in mine.

Plenty of stories for when we're old and gray
Arise and drink your bliss!

"I think I really did wake up in a fairy tale today," I said to Adrian.

"Or perhaps you're still in my arms, dreaming a wonderful dream."

Keep reading for a preview of SOFTER THAN STEEL, the next book in the Love and Steel series!

RICK

RIDING THE WAVE

Seventeen thousand fans can't be wrong.

Rick Rottenberg clipped his mic into its stand, lifted his face to the spots and hazers shining high above the Palais Omnisports de Paris-Bercy stage, and threw his head back, exalted.

Sweat-soaked ringlets grazed the middle of his slick bare back. It had taken four years to grow his hair back out to acceptable headbanging, rock-and-roll length. Running a hand through the dark, unruly mass of curls, he smiled. Sometimes he forgot it was there, even dreamed his head was still shaved clean. He had kept it shorn like a Buddhist monk for so long, first in solidarity for Simone, then for years after for no reason he could ascertain.

Simone's gone.

Gone.

Even in a sea of thousands, you're alone.

Grimacing, he hoisted his guitar by its neck, high overhead.

The crowd's response was visceral. A rolling current of fists raised, eyes squeezed shut, and a collective hoarse roar emanated from their throats. Rick ripped out his in-ear monitors by their cords, letting the sound hit his eardrums full-force.

Like bracing himself for a hard wave, he took a wide stance in his black leather boots and steeled himself.

I was born to do this.

It was less a thought and more like a full-on sensory experience, as his eyes adjusted to the raised house lights and his ears welcomed the cacophony of applause. Dry ice from the fog machines burned his nose, and the ten-gauge steel of the guitar strings cut into his palm as he used his instrument like a conductor's baton to whip the French crowd into a frenzied cyclone.

And he tasted victory.

It had taken four years. But Riff Rotten was back.

Because seventeen thousand screaming, rabid, shining, elated metal fans can't be wrong.

Right?

He flicked a look side-stage toward the large digital clock sitting on top of the monitor engineer's board. There was still a good eight-minute block for the band to get one last song in before the venue's strict eleven p.m. curfew. But as he turned to his right to suggest it to Digger, he noticed his bandmate exiting the stage. The only encore that interested his lead guitarist was the one waiting for him in the wings.

Kat.

Rick turned away as Adrian grinned like she was the winning lottery ticket and swung her around in a gravity-defying hug.

From his place at center stage, Rick had barely noticed Kat down in the pit tonight, but Adrian obviously had. *He's always been the one to care about the details,* Rick reminded himself. *You're about the big picture.* That's how they'd always functioned.

Or how we malfunctioned, as the case may be.

Corroded Corpse was now back and at the top of their game as the Rotten Graves Project. And Digger Graves was more interested in picking china patterns than tremolo picking his guitar and melting the fans' faces off.

His timing was certainly crap, wasn't it?

The neck of Rick's Gibson slipped through his fatigued and sweaty fingers. In a burst of pent-up energy, he gripped it close to the headstock with both hands and pinwheeled the axe through the air. Sam froze to his left. The bassist had at least had the decency to come downstage for a bow. Now he took a step back and cast a wary glance at Jim, who was leaning over his drum kit.

Guitar met stage floor with a loud crack, like a gunshot. Wood flew and guitar strings popped as Rick pulled it high overhead, sliced it through the air, and smashed it down again and again, to the left, to the right. Jim popped back behind his kit and provided a rising crescendo of cymbals to accompany each upward move and kicked his double bass drum in perfect pace each time Rick's guitar made contact: with the floor, the riser, the amps behind him, and the wedges in front of him. Sam did a little hop as the entire body of the Gibson Memphis guitar separated from the neck and slid toward him.

The kids in the crowd had lost their bloody minds by then.

RICK CLICKED the pause button on his laptop and dragged the bar of the video back so he could watch himself lift the jagged broken neck of his guitar like a conquering hero wielding his sword victoriously—eyes wild, bare chest heaving—while tonight's crowd screamed its approval. Judging from the dozen or so fan-shot videos that had hit YouTube by midnight, his little spectacle had looked pretty damn good from the audience's point of view.

Leaning back in the hotel's desk chair, he twisted his lips into a sardonic smile, shook his glass to loosen up the ice, and took a sip. The single malt's buttery burn was welcome in his whiskey tonight. Subtle notes of orange peel, burnt caramel, and clove teased his tongue and promised to bring the noise in his head down to a dull roar.

The trill of his room phone summoned him. Padding barefoot across the lush carpeting of his Mandarin Oriental suite, he silenced it by placing it to his ear.

Isabelle needed no salutation to get the conversation going. The band's publicist launched into her tirade unprompted.

"So what was with that little hissy fit on stage tonight, huh?"

"*Bonsoir,* Isabelle. *Comment allez-vous?*"

"Don't play cute and French with me, mister."

Rick picked out brash notes of trash talk, Salem Ultra Lights, and Brooklyn in her voice. *Not nearly as smooth as whiskey on the palate,* he thought, wincing as she doused his ear with her version of twenty questions. And label expectations. And SoundScan numbers. And ticket sales. And who's not returning her calls, and who needs to do some serious ass-kissing now that payola bribes were no longer in style.

Rick drained his whiskey glass, but felt completely sober. What had happened to the promise he and Digger made four years ago under the roof of Madison Square Garden? *Of doing things our way,* he asked himself, *this time around?*

He should've known better. This was the music business, after all. Emphasis on *business.* You could have all the talent and drive, but you needed that army behind you. The minute the two of them had buried the hatchet and agreed to play that reunion show, the armies had assembled and performed a coup d'état. The booking agent, the record label, groupies, and hangers-on had all awoken from what appeared to be an enchanted slumber, as if the last twenty years had passed for them in the blink of an eye. Business as usual.

Only their former publicist/self-appointed interim Queen

of Everything had awoken crankier than a disturbed hornets' nest.

If she hadn't been Simone's best friend since childhood, Rick probably would've called the exterminator to fog Isabelle out of his life ages ago.

"Behave yourself, finish the goddamn run, and get your ass back to the States in one piece," Isabelle commanded. "Simone's parents are counting on you for the hospital wing dedication. Then we've got the one-offs in L.A. and Chicago, your Rock and Roll Hall of Fame appearance, and the Northeast leg to get through yet. And two months of lockout booked in the studio here. Oh, and the mayor's office has finally given us the green light for the outdoor video shoot."

"Relax, Isabelle. We've got it under control."

We. The bloody band. Not you.

"Says the guy who just broke a three-thousand-dollar guitar on stage? Yeah. Okay." There was a forced exhale, and Rick bet the bank she was standing on her penthouse balcony, flicking ashes down on the heads of the plebs who dared troll her Upper East Side neighborhood. "And where the hell is Adrian? Would it kill him to return a phone call once in a while?"

"Indisposed."

Rick rubbed his temple, contemplating another glass or the five hours' sleep he could catch before the bus came to pick up the band. He didn't care to contemplate what Adrian and Kat were up to in their fancy hotel suite down the hall at this hour.

"Yeah? What's his drug of choice these days?"

Would you believe me if I said a widowed librarian and her eight-year-old daughter? "Nothing."

"I wasn't born yesterday, Rick."

"And neither was Adrian. In fact, he was born forty-five years ago, this day. It's his birthday. So let's all leave him the fuck alone, shall we?" The sarcasm did a number on his throat, way worse than the whiskey.

"Let me guess." Isabelle gave a dignified snort. "Kat showed up at the show tonight to surprise him?" She barely paused to let Rick respond before throwing out her "Tell me you're not jealous?" card.

Even though he was an ocean away, Rick kept a poker face and his own hand close to his chest.

Whatever the answer was, he sure as hell wouldn't find it in this long-distance phone call, or in the melting ice at the bottom of his whiskey glass.

"Don't ask him to choose," she warned. "You will lose."

"Isabelle. As much as I'd love to listen to you recite more poetic words of wisdom to me, I'm going to—"

"*He* never asked *you* to choose between the band and Simone."

"I'm going to hang up now," Rick finished quietly.

Whether Isabelle responded or not, he'd never know. The roaring in his ears had come back full force. But it wasn't the hordes of screaming masses this time around. It was the roar of the ocean, back home in Hawaii.

He reeled back to 1988, standing with Simone on Kauai's Polihale beach on the westernmost shore. Miles and miles of deserted sand, mostly due to the fierce currents. He had stood on that beach for what seemed like hours, staring at the incredible sand dunes and the cliffs of the Na Pali.

And had experienced his first, full-blown panic attack.

"It's the kind of place that makes one realize how insignificant one really is in the grand scheme of things," he liked to tell people. "Pulled my ego down a few pegs and got my priorities in line straightaway." With the band just a smoking wreck of its former self, he and Simone had relocated to the island with the children shortly after, and family became his number one priority.

Rick was hobbled by the memory, and his legs threatened mutiny as he careened to the bathroom.

"He didn't have to ask me," he said aloud to the mirror, as if he needed to convince the somber dark eyes staring back at him. "I made the choice myself."

His reflection grimly broke the news: *Too late.*

Simone was dead within six years.

He gripped the vanity in front of him as the blackness of the memory washed over him, like it always did. *Keep your head,* he commanded himself now, although he remembered going totally off his nut at the time. The locals had talked about the powerful Polihale heiau, a sacred site believed to be one of the points from which the souls of the dead departed the island into the setting sun. It sounded so beautiful, so peaceful. He had wanted to go and die there, to travel with her. The kids had been the only things holding him back.

The thought of his boys buoyed and anchored him still. All three were now grown up and out in the world on their own. Armed with five college degrees among them, they'd each flown the coop upon graduation without ever looking back.

And what would they have seen had they even bothered?

Rick pulled back his curls from his face with one hand and splashed cool water across his heated cheeks. Face dripping, he let his hair drop into place and contemplated what he saw in the mirror before him. Rangy limbs, their muscles lean from swinging eight pounds of guitar night after night. The strong jut of his jaw, with its dark bristle of five o'clock shadow emerging. Sharp angles where cheekbones met the hollows under his tired eyes. Under his wild mane of charcoal hair, a heavy, determined brow just starting to show the weathered lines of a worrier, aged forty-four this spring.

Father.

Widower.

Rocker.

Empty nester.

His dark brows lifted at that preposterous thought. *How*

could that be? The contradiction in terms describing this current phase of his life brought him back to the present, all threats of his usual, full-blown panic attack abated. He hadn't had one since leaving Hawaii three weeks ago. *So much for that track record.* But the tension eased and a strange sigh of relief blew through his lips.

The storm had passed, for the moment.

Now what?

Sleep. Bus. Show. Repeat. He had no problem jumping through the hoops of the rock and roll traveling circus.

It was the looming prospect of time off the road that terrified him.

RICK

DON'T BREAK THE OATH

*O*NE MORE DOWN, *here we go. Another town, another show.*

Rick found Adrian backstage in the band's hospitality room in Barcelona, signing black-and-white press pictures in rapid succession. Sharpie marker barely made contact as his hand moved fluidly, his thumb sliding each photo aside before his trademark scrawl had even dried on the page. Jim, who appeared to be building the world's tallest sandwich from the catering deli tray, would stop his task every few seconds to retrieve a photo that escaped to the floor.

"Aren't those the signed promo photos the French label wanted?" Sam asked.

He and Martin, their tour manager, had just returned from a Starbucks run. Some things stayed consistent on the road, and finding the Seattle coffee chain was one of them. It didn't matter the currency or language, one could always order an overpriced Americano and get just that.

"Yeah. Martin can mail them back," Adrian said, scratching an itch on his cheek with the capped end of the Sharpie before getting back to work.

"But weren't you the one who insisted we get them done and out of the way last night?" Sam demanded.

The three others had done their share of signing, cramping their hands before the Paris show, while Adrian had promised to do his straightaway after the gig was over. Anger built within Rick as he watched the photos spread themselves across the entire countertop.

Turned out Adrian had had another itch to scratch last night.

"He was too busy with his pit kitten," Rick said, barely able to keep the contempt out of his voice.

Last night they had been in the midst of a blistering dual bridge toward the end of the second set, playing in perfect guitar-mony, neither missing a lick. Suddenly, Adrian started shredding even faster, harder, and more passionately than it seemed possible, leaving Rick completely in the dust. Rick had followed his line of vision and spied his bandmate's prize front and center. Sweat had streamed rivers toward Adrian's grin as he just shook his head slowly in disbelief, the crowd's cacophony reaching an eardrum-splitting crescendo as he wound down to meet the rhythm of Rick and the rest of the band to play the final verse.

"Kat? A pit kitten?" Adrian sputtered a laugh. "Hardly." The glaze of his ice blue eyes denoted his mind was in a far more delightful place.

Yes, Rick could see the appeal of the small-town librarian. The cascade of chestnut hair, the alabaster skin. But it was her eyes, those bright green jewels, that took you beyond the surface. Wit and warmth were sexy tools operated by an expert engineer suited up in a body that wouldn't quit.

What the hell had Kat been thinking? A metal show was a full-contact sport up front. It was a mosh pit down there, Rick thought darkly. Not a coffee klatch. She didn't belong on that side of the barrier.

All evening, security guards had plucked sweaty, battered fans over the railing from the vise grip of center stage. Kat had indicated it was her turn and, with the help of her fellow mates in the trench, she had been lifted up, up, and over. Adrian had signaled to a second guard, who escorted her to the inner sanctum of backstage rather than just expelling her safely back onto the floor. She hadn't even brought her laminate.

Fancy that, someone we know actually buying a ticket for one of our shows. Thanks to Jim's and Sam's social butterfly tendencies, the guest list had begun to grow exponentially every night since the reunion.

"Seeing her down there gave you quite the hard-on, I'm sure."

"Bigger than the one you got from smashing that vintage Gibson," Adrian lobbed right back.

Sam choked on his six-euro cup of coffee, although of the three witnesses in the room, he was the one most familiar with Adrian and Rick's witty brand of bandied insults.

"Right, I'm sure you put yours to good use last night. Giving your groupie her twelve-hundred-dollar orgasm."

Chatter in the room ceased at Rick's comment. All that could be heard was Jim's cold cut hitting bread with a wet slap.

Adrian calmly resumed his task. "How do you figure, mate?" The marker squeaked across another glossy photo as everyone else in the room held their collective breath.

"Let's see: her first-class plane ticket to Paris, the five-star hotel room, the car and driver . . ." Rick ticked them off on his fingers. He knew the expense meant nothing to Adrian. Nor to Kat, compared to witnessing the dawn of recognition on Adrian's face. Surprising her fiancé by showing up for one night in the middle of his band's European tour to celebrate his forty-fifth birthday had probably been, as the MasterCard commercials say, priceless. But Rick couldn't help himself. "Still paying for sex after all these years, Digger?"

Whether it was because of the sneering use of his stage name or the reference to his debauched behavior from decades back, Adrian's patience had clearly thinned to the point of breaking.

Just one more crack—

"I know exactly what you want me to do." In a flash, Adrian was all up in his grill, as his sons would say. Platform boots brought Adrian nose to nose with Rick. "You want me to take a swing, to hit you, so we'll be even." He shook his shaggy blond head of hair, even let a ghost of a smile slip through. "Not gonna happen, mate."

It was Rick who felt the chill through his veins, as the realization sunk in and doused him with icy shame.

"How about you write a song about *my* future wife, have it hit the charts with a bullet, and *I'll* take credit for it? Maybe then we'll be even, huh?" Adrian finished.

From the corner of his eye, Rick saw Sam and Jim exchange a look. He knew what they were thinking. Far be it from Rick to write *any* song, much less a chart-topping song like the one Adrian had penned about Simone so long ago.

Adrian, after all, was all about the details. And Rick, the big picture.

Sanitize my insanity . . . cleanse me, make me whole again, Simone . . .

Darkness loomed, threatening his vision with a fade to black.

Oh ruddy fecking hell.

It was no wonder writer's block had chased him from coast to coast, the muse eluding him both on and off-stage. In an unspoken decree as the King of Doom, Rick had forbidden the band's greatest hit to appear on any set list henceforth. Since reuniting, nobody had dared address the lingering ghost in the room.

Until now.

"I'll have no school yard squabbles on my watch," Martin boomed, "not while I have Isabelle back in the States to reckon with!" His Scottish burr was very apparent. "She'll mop the floor with the lot of us." All six and a half feet and fifteen stone of their tour manager quivered at the utterance of her name. "You'll take the stage in ten, you'll play the poxy gig, and when the tour is done, you two can go your separate ways. Understood?"

Adrian sputtered a laugh. "As if it were that simple! Rick's let Isabelle sell us into indentured servitude. VIP packages, meet and greets, Rock and Roll Fantasy Camp, and propping us up in the Hall of Fame museum like the bloody relics we are, before prodding us like cattle right into the studio. It never ends!"

"Is that what you want, then? For the whole thing to be over with again?" Another wave of anxiety rolled up Rick's frame as he stared his oldest friend down.

Adrian should want for nothing, he thought. *With his instant American family waiting for him back home. But me?*

"Enough," Sam hollered, startling everyone. "It could be worse. It *has* been worse. Remember Cass? Remember Wren?" Everyone bowed their heads at the memory of their fallen crewmate, and scuffed their soles at the mention of Corroded Corpse's wretched ex-manager, who left them broken down in his dust. "It's better now. Because it's ours to make it better, yeah? No one else's."

He plucked the Sharpie out of Adrian's clenched fist and foisted it upon Rick. "Your turn to write the set list, Rotten."

THE BAND EXPLODED across the stage in a myriad of lights as Jim's machine-gun drum fills ricocheted through the arena. Sam was up prowling the catwalks, slapping sound out of his bass to the roar of the audience. Opening with "Blood Oath" was always a solid crowd-pleaser, Rick thought as he and Adrian galloped through the intro like a well-oiled machine. Although his excuses and apologies had lodged stubbornly in his throat backstage, he now exorcised them through glass-shatteringly high screams and unwavering, crisp lyrics to the song he and his best friend had penned as school chums.

Adrian's fist rose in solidarity with the masses sprawled below, and one of the movers from the lighting truss overhead highlighted the raised scar on his inner arm. They had been just boys, hopped up on Norse mythology and the idea of *að blanda blóði saman*—"to mix blood together." Rick flicked a glance at the hollow of his own elbow, to the identical mark hatched there.

Blood brothers.

A storm of emotion gathered deep in Rick's chest, and on its bare surface, the thin, simple misericorde dagger tattooed there rose and fell, rose and fell, as he belted out the final chorus to "Blood Oath," of promises kept and tears wept.

A bump to his shoulder told him Adrian had come to share the microphone under the spotlight of center stage. Rick leaned into him, his bare back coming into contact with Adrian's leather-clad one as their fingers scurried across the frets of their guitars, playing rhythm and lead. Beneath the vest he wore, the twin to Rick's dagger graced Adrian's skin, and he breathed life into it as he sang in unison with his blood brother.

We bear some of the same scars, Rick thought, matching Digger's smile with a genuine one of his own as they made peace with a high five of their headstocks and strutted back to their respective spaces on stage.

Sharing war wounds, like the brothers in the song who loved each other dearly, yet hated each other fiercely.

But some we must carry alone.

SIDRA
BEATLES OR ROLLING STONES

SIDRA SULLIVAN DROPPED herself and her yoga bag down at the table recently bussed clean by her brother, heaving out a potent sigh. *Thank nirvana for the Naked Bagel.* Although their linguist father might argue otherwise, there was a portmanteau for what she felt: *hangry.* It was the impatient and emotional intersection of hungry and angry.

She needed food and serenity—now.

"You know, if you keep showing up here like this, Sid, my boss is going to name a bagel after you." Seamus turned both his ball cap and a chair backward. *Such a guy thing to do,* Sidra thought as her brother pushed the hat down on his thick blond locks with the flat of his large palm before straddling the seat across from her.

At the moment, she was completely disgusted with all guys and their moves.

Although Seamus, to his credit, had at least given her the best table in the house.

"Too late!" Liz breezed out from behind the counter, rocking a tight black T-shirt that proclaimed *Bagels. What's Your Excuse?* "One Manhattan Goddess bagel, on the house." With a flick of her wrist, she set Sidra's plate spinning down in front of her.

"You know, if you keep giving freebies to your friends, you're going to go broke," Sidra called, but Liz's back, sporting *Go Naked or Go Home* in bold red lettering, had already turned. "Let me pay, for once! I want you to take my money."

"Too bad!" Liz trilled. She had already rocketed herself back behind the counter, slicing a half 18 dozen to go for the next customer in line before Sidra could even reach into her bag.

"Here," she said to her brother, palming a twenty into his hand. "Go make me a taro bubble tea and put the change in the tip jar."

She had no idea what Liz's rent was like for the Naked Bagel, but she could only imagine it hiked higher with every street sign here on the Upper East Side of Manhattan.

And just like with Evolve, Sidra's yoga studio on the Lower East Side, every little bit counted. Seamus pocketed the soft, worn Andrew Jackson in his apron with a grin. Sidra knew her brother was as honest as the day was long, but he couldn't resist trying to rile her up.

"And don't be a scammer," she added, cocking a dark brow in his direction as he sauntered toward the cash register.

Sidra was pretty fed up with those, too.

Using the length of orange ribbon she never left home without, she tied her glossy black ponytail tight and high and inhaled deeply, relishing the nutty fragrance of the toasted sunflower bagel. It was studded with flax and filled to bursting with albacore tuna and smooth, ripe avocado. Indeed a treat fit for a goddess, and as the shirt Seamus was wearing boasted, *Happiness Is a Warm Bagel.*

"Which one, Sis? Fab Four or Glimmer Twins?"

Seamus held a fistful of bills and coins over the two tip jars on the counter. Like the workers' shirts, the sayings on the jars were clever and changed daily.

"Both," she managed around a mouthful of bagel.

He dropped the bills into the Beatles' jar and the change into the Rolling Stones' jar with a melodic clunk, and then went to work on her tea. Sidra watched as owner and right-hand man swerved around each other in the tight space behind the counter, tossing, reaching, and calling out to each other as they sailed through what was left of the lingering late-lunch crowd. It was like a fluid ballet: Seamus's muscular bronze arms shooting past Liz's pale freckled ones, working in synchronicity.

"Delivery to 55th and Lex," Liz commanded, shoving brown-bagged orders down the counter. "Then the usual two dozen to the doctor's office on York." She relieved him of Sidra's bubble tea and righted his ball cap. "Sixteenth floor."

Sidra had already polished off the first half of her sandwich and was contemplating its equally tempting twin. Teaching always worked up her appetite, especially the free lunch break yoga class she sometimes led at a nearby park. Although her hunger pangs had diminished considerably, her anger and disgust still lingered after this afternoon's episode.

"So, what gives?" Liz plunked herself into the chair Seamus had vacated and slid the pale purple drink across the table.

"Ech. Guys." Sidra swiped a hand in front of her face as if the entire male race were a cloud of gnats annoying her. "Why do they have to be such dogs?"

Liz took a quick scan of tables around them before allowing her mossy green eyes to meet Sidra's brown ones. The lunch crowd had officially dissipated, it seemed she could finally relax.

"Come on, can you blame them? You're standing there with your tight little body, telling them to assume the position. Down dog, up dog . . . Trade that mat for a flogger and you could be dominatrix of all the dogs." She twirled Sidra's abandoned straw wrapper around a finger and added with a devilish wink, "Probably make a helluva lot more money, too."

"Seriously, Sid. Time to grow up and get a *real* job." Seamus grinned, clipping on his space-age-looking bike helmet.

Sidra gave a snort. "Says the guy about to pedal across town with bagels in his basket."

"Bagels that aren't getting any younger, or warmer," Liz added. "Get going, you." She pointed to the front door. "Let us have our girl talk."

"See ya back at the ranch, Sid." Seamus dropped a kiss on the top of her silky head.

"So," Liz said. "Where were we? Oh yeah. Floggers." She snuck a bite of the bagel from Sidra's plate.

"I'm serious. Male yoga teachers probably don't have to put up with this shit."

After five years of teaching every type of yoga across three different boroughs, Sidra thought she had heard every pickup line, from *Hey, I've got a yoga mat built for two,* to *Gee, I bet you could bounce a quarter off that asana!* Frowning, she stabbed her straw at the fat black pearls of tapioca at the bottom of her bubble tea. "Let's just say this guy thought getting in touch with his inner self gave him license to touch me."

"That's not a dog, that's a fucking pig." Finally, Liz was appropriately outraged. "It's not you. And it's not yoga. It's Manhattan. What do we expect, living on an island two miles wide and thirteen miles long?"

"Is that why you're dating a guy who lives twenty-eight hundred miles away?" Sidra teased.

"As if." Liz gave a snort. "Hardly ideal." She sighed, folding the thin wrapper and squeezing it between her thumb and forefinger like a tiny paper accordion. "I'm telling you, this borough's run dry. All the good guys here are spoken for. Or gay. Time to import some new ones."

Sidra chewed on a boba thoughtfully. Liz made it sound easy, like heading down the Jersey Turnpike to IKEA. Sidra didn't want to settle for quick, cheap, and some assembly required. She wanted a drama-free relationship that would stand the test of time, with a solid, decent guy. Was that so wrong?

Yeah, but would you even recognize him if he came along?

The last time Sidra went to IKEA for something practical, like a rug, she ended up coming home with a single bar stool and a string of lights shaped like margarita glasses. Hardly sensible. Hell, she couldn't even choose between the Beatles and the Rolling Stones.

"Could we at least export a few of the bad ones," Sidra joked, "and even out the dating pool?"

Bells above the bagel shop's door clanged, grabbing both women's attentions.

"Anyway, like I'm one to talk." Liz stood and brushed invisible crumbs off her apron-covered miniskirt. "Kevin's true love is his restaurant. He's been talking about moving back east for four years already. I'm beginning to think he only bothers to enter my zip code when his favorite band comes to town. It's starting to give me a complex."

Now it was Sidra's turn to snort. At least Liz's zip code was seeing some occasional action. Ever since Sidra had kicked Charlie out, the only action she got in her zip code was self-addressed, so to speak.

"Be thankful he's just a fan of the band and not in it. Talk about being married to the job," Sidra grumbled. The road had been Charlie's bride for years, and she had had to settle for being mistress muse. "Musicians are the worst."

Liz ducked back behind the counter. "I'm hardly the authority," she began, wielding her huge serrated knife, "but I'd like to think that chivalry isn't quite yet dead." With that, she lopped an everything bagel in half and anointed it with a schmear of cream cheese.

"Oh, sh—" Liz bit her lip, censoring herself in the customers' presence. "Seamus!" She groaned at the sight of the lumpy brown bag still sitting on the counter. "Your flaky brother forgot to take half the order!"

"No worries, I'll take them," Sidra offered.

"Seriously? That would help tremendously. I'm down a guy. I would take them myself, but . . ." She jotted down the address on an order pad and thrust it at Sidra. "I owe you a solid, big-time."

"Well, I owed *you* for my last ten bagels. So we're even." She smiled.

"You sure you have time? It's a bit of a maze in there. Huge medical complex."

"I'm sure. My beginners class downtown isn't till five." Sidra grabbed her yoga bag and the warm order of fresh bagels.

"Still rocking that senior set, huh?"

"You know it." She waved. Actually, Sidra didn't mind teaching the geriatric group that often showed up for her Monday beginners class at Evolve Yoga. They didn't show off, they didn't hit on her, and they were open to new poses. She smiled as she crossed Lexington, remembering how her class had mastered Lizard last week. Age spots and crepe paper–like skin had lent themselves well to the pose.

Lizard pose always reminded Sidra of Charlie's iguana. Banana Louie was the only thing she truly missed about her ex-boyfriend. She used to get nervous when Charlie would let the creature roam free in her apartment. A lash from its powerful tail could easily draw blood or break one of her mother's few remaining sculptures. But with time, she came to like watching Banana Louie. Especially when he'd bask under his UVB bulb and let her feed him green beans.

Turned out Charlie was the one you had to look out for. Chasing tail and biting the hand that fed him. Turning wild when given the allowance to roam free.

Dark thoughts swept in as she crossed 64th Street, clouding

Sidra's mind and tightening her chest. *Set your best intention for the day,* she told herself. *Just let it go.*

Maybe chivalry isn't dead, Sidra reasoned as she breezed through the door of the medical center. *Maybe it's just being kept on life support somewhere. Waiting for the right person to come along and breathe life into it.*

Or to pull the plug and put it out of its misery.

RICK

SHAFTED

RICK SURVEYED the crowd before him, clearing his throat loudly. Discordant chatter fell to an expectant hush, and all eyes were on him. Camera flashes popped.

I don't belong here.

A prod in the back from Isabelle reminded Rick that this wasn't about him.

He looked down at his hands and almost burst out laughing. It was like one of those horrible dreams you had as a kid, showing up at school and suddenly realizing you're naked. Except he was way overdressed, in a bespoke suit with a horrible Brioni tie strangling him in ways his guitar strap never could.

But that sinking feeling of the dream, of looking down to the utter shock of nakedness? Yeah, that was there. He had no guitar to hide behind. But what he did have in his hands was a pair of gigantic, ceremonial scissors.

"Don't hurt yourself," Isabelle wisecracked from behind him.

"Right." He knew the drill. Welcome everyone, allow the hospital president to say a few words, shake hands for the camera, cut the blasted thing, and call it a day. Both his publicist and the hospital's spokesperson had been over it ad nauseam.

He opened his mouth and words started to flow. But the audience began to murmur again, shaking their heads and raising brows to one another.

"Sorry, sorry." He tapped the dead microphone, then remedied it with a flick of the switch. "It's been a long time since I've had to sound-check my own mic," he joked. "Check, check one-two." That garnered a laugh, mainly from the under forty crowd.

Rick had done the easy stuff earlier. Posing for pictures with various board of director muckety-mucks, signing autographs for them and for some of the doctors, their children, and their children's children. Now came the hard part. He glanced down at the wide, orange satin ribbon stretched out before him as Isabelle gave him another nudge. It was the only thing keeping him from performing a perfect swan dive into the arms of the city officials and dignitaries seated below.

That and social decorum, he supposed.

"Thank you all for coming, and for giving me this honor. Simone would be . . ."

Simone would be what?

Rick glanced around at the shiny new cancer wing of the famed Manhattan hospital. His wife had died far away from here, the city of her birth, and from her parents, who had been unable to make the opening due to unforeseen circumstances. They were the ones who tirelessly raised the money and spoke for the cause, year after bloody year. He was just another checkbook, a token figurehead. Putting money where his mouth—or daresay where his heart—was not. He certainly didn't deserve this honor that had fallen upon him right in the middle of his band's tour, yanking him from the promise of the road and back to the crapshoot of reality.

"Simone would be . . ."

As he searched for the right words, the devil riding shotgun on the shoulder seam of his designer suit provided some choice ones.

Simone would be here if it weren't for you, you pompous, self-centered prick.

His fists clenched, and he heard the crisp bite of stainless steel cutting through the satin. The orange bits fluttered to either side of him, and he stepped back, feeling faint. A collective gasp emanated from below and the president gaped uselessly, unread speech gripped in his hand. Isabelle was at the podium now, not a hair out of place and smiling as the crowd recovered and politely clapped.

"I have to get out of here," Rick hissed at the back of her perfumed neck, "or I'm going to lose it."

"Fine. Go. Take the service elevator," she replied, mouth still frozen in her happy publicist's smile. Isabelle was on the board of the Simone Banquet Memorial Foundation and was certainly equipped to provide the lip service for it. "There's a car waiting downstairs to take you back to the airport."

She relieved him of the Goliath shears and planted what felt like the kiss of Judas on his cheek. Exposing him for what he really was. Why, why, *why* did he let her talk him into this?

Rick bounded behind the pipe and drape toward the old part of the hospital, away from the Simone Banquet Memorial Cancer Center wing that he had just prematurely dedicated.

Why had he even bothered to come? He was useless at these types of things. Beyond useless, actually, and tipping over into the hazardous category. God, he couldn't get out of here fast enough. He should be safely on the other coast with the band in Los Angeles, not here. Anywhere but here. Fingers worked to loosen the tight knot at his throat as he proceeded down the hallway toward the service elevator, which was miraculously opening at that very moment to allow a worker off.

"Hold the lift!" he barked as the doors began to close upon his approach. He saw no one inside move a finger in response. "Dammit!" Curse New York and its bloody New York minute, with everyone rushing and no one taking the time—

A slim, tan leg shot through the gap in the doors, causing them to spring open again.

Rick murmured his thanks as he wormed in, past the tiny sandal dangling from the foot holding the door at bay.

"Crap. My flip-flop!"

The owner of the leg shifted a huge paper sack of heavenly smelling baked goods in her arms, just in time to catch a glimpse of her shoe slipping neatly through the crack as the doors slid shut with a smug *ding*.

"Son of a bitch!"

The expletive hardly matched the wisp of a girl who had uttered it. She had the delicate features of a china doll and barely came up to Rick's chest. Yet he and the other occupants of the elevator cowered as she swore like a trucker.

"Sorry," was all Rick could muster.

"Me too." The girl glared at him with eyes startlingly bright, banded in colors that reminded Rick of the tiger iron stone he used to bring back as gifts for his sons after tour stops in Australia. She mumbled something about good deeds unpunished and left it at that.

As they rode in uncomfortable silence, Rick realized the elevator was going up, not down. He had been so intent on escaping, the thought hadn't even occurred to him that it might not be going the way he wanted.

Nothing was going the way he wanted these days.

He sighed, his eyes drifting down. The girl was balanced like a stork, her bare foot nestled against the inner thigh of her opposite leg. How she was able to stand like that while the elevator took its time to stop at every other floor, Rick had no clue. Not that he could blame her; he wouldn't want his skin coming into contact with any part of Manhattan's terra firma, whether inside or out. Her arms were still clutching the huge bag. Rick caught a whiff of cinnamon swirling with honey and walnuts and realized he had not eaten since landing on American soil.

An older woman in pink scrubs commandeering a cart full of hospital supplies finally spoke up. "Here, *chica.*" She rummaged through the items on the bottom shelf of the cart. "You take," she continued in her broken English, smiling and offering up a scrunched handful of something.

Without a word to Rick, the girl handed off her bag to him so she could slide what looked like a pale blue paper shoe over her bare foot.

"*Gracias,*" she said politely and pointedly to the woman. Which seemed to imply *No thanks to you* as far as Rick was concerned. She was a firecracker, this one.

Pink Scrubs got off at the next floor, leaving just the two of them on board. She took back custody of her bagels and kept her eyes on the lighted panel above the door. The only number left lit was sixteen, and they were almost there. Rick leaned past her to press L, feeling like an idiot. *L for Loser.* The girl smirked but didn't comment.

Her hair was straight and glossy, darker than even his, and caught back in a ribbon the same orange hue as the one he had just snipped in half back in the multi-million-dollar wing that bore his wife's name. He had felt so useless earlier. Now he had the sudden urge to do something, say something, to remedy the current situation.

"Can I buy you a coffee?" he blurted. *Lame.* "A new shoe?" That earned him a roll of those tiger iron eyes, flecked with golden jasper and bits as dark as black hematite. "How about a tetanus shot?"

With a dismissive snort, she scuffed down the hall in one paper shoe and didn't look back.

SIDRA
CINDERELLA IN REVERSE

Do a good deed and what do you get? Sidra thought. *The shaft.* Literally.

Truth be told, she had been too busy sneaking a glance at the gorgeous specimen who had entered the tight quarters of the elevator to notice her silly shoe was falling off her foot.

And that accent. Talk about imported!

Guys in power suits usually intimidated her, but something about this guy was different. Make no mistake—he absolutely owned the look. Especially with that cascade of long hair. The unexpected contradiction made him even more intriguing.

His suit had appeared tailor-made for his body, and that tie screamed spendy. Sidra would bet the last bagel in her bag that his shoes were a) Italian and b) worth more than her whole wardrobe combined. Not that her wardrobe contained much more than yoga pants and sports bras, but still. His shoes were really nice. Way too expensive (*and whoa—big!*) to ever lose down an elevator shaft.

She thought back to her "where have all the good guys gone?" conversation with Liz. *Gay?* Maybe. *Taken?* Maybe that, too. He had had a faint but fresh-looking lipstick mark on his cheekbone, she had noticed. Shoot. Oh well.

Sidra delivered the bag of bagels left behind by Seamus with little fanfare. The receptionist even gave her a tip. Enough for the subway ride home, but since she only had one damn shoe, she'd have to spring for a cab. No way was she going to deal with the hassle of the MTA while a paper bootie was cinched to her ankle.

Mr. Import had offered to treat her to a tetanus shot. Cute.

And she totally blew him off for his trouble. *Nice one, Sid. You may as well have given Manhattan's last knight in shining armor the finger.*

She wondered if he was a doctor. Plenty of them seemed to have abandoned the white coats these days. And the way he carried himself gave the impression he was some sort of big cheese, compared to the other lab rats in the maze of a medical center. But why the hell had he been riding the service elevator? Sidra knew why she was on it. Upon checking in at the front desk, she had been relegated to taking the route reserved for deliveries and dirty laundry. Certainly not the preferred mode of transportation for someone so well dressed.

The clap-scuff of her hurried pace echoed through the empty hall. *Back to the scene of the crime,* she thought as the elevator doors slid open.

"Your chariot awaits."

Mr. Import was back, and he had brought a wheelchair.

"You've got to be kidding me." Sidra laughed self-consciously. She hoped the Manhattan Goddess bagel hadn't given her tuna breath.

"It's the least I can do." He pointed to the seat. "In you go."

Sidra humored him. Maybe he could roll her down to the taxi stand, at least.

"Do you make a habit of this?" she asked.

"Of what? Absconding with hospital property?" As his

laugh rumbled above her, she wished she hadn't taken the seat so she could see the smile that went with it. Like his suit, she bet it looked like a million bucks. "Hardly."

"No, of riding the dirty service elevator all day."

They passed by two more floors before he answered. "Only when there's the possibility of rescue and redemption." The handsome stranger's stilted murmur was close to her ear, raising goose bumps and questions she didn't dare ask.

The ride going down was fast and smooth, with no stops in between. He whisked the wheelchair into the busy lobby and finessed his way to the sliding glass doors, humming something in a melodic baritone as he pushed.

"Okay, well. The ride stops here. I'm fine, thanks." She really needed to get downtown so she could grab another pair of shoes from home and hoof it to the studio. "I'm going to be late for work."

"Well, you certainly can't go to work barefoot."

Now it was Sidra's turn to laugh as she accepted his large hand and allowed herself to be helped out of the wheelchair. "Actually, I can."

He raised one heavy, sculpted eyebrow. "Look. You said no to my offer of coffee—"

"And to your offer of immunization," Sidra interjected.

"—so let me at least replace your shoe. I insist." He was already signaling to a—no joke—long, black limousine idling out front. Its driver popped out and stepped lively toward the back door.

"Dude. I'm not getting in a car with a total stranger. Sorry."

Mr. Import's dark brow furrowed as if he didn't quite understand. He *so* wasn't from around here. "You're not getting in a car with a total stranger, you're getting into a car with . . ."

"James, sir." The driver tapped his own name tag with a smile.

"You're getting in a car with James." He turned to the driver and Sidra saw the flash of a bill disappear into the liveryman's breast pocket as they spoke in hushed tones. "James is going to take you to a shoe store, and then he's going to take you to work." Now Sidra caught a glimpse of his smile, which appeared to be tinged with the tiniest bit of regret. "I've actually got a plane to catch."

Sidra watched from the open window of the limo as Mr. Import stepped to the curb and raised his arm. "JFK Airport, please," she heard him say.

So, chivalry isn't dead after all, she thought. *It's hailing a yellow medallion cab to Queens.*

"THERE'S A DUANE READE." Sidra pointed, but James appeared to have strict orders to not stop until he had reached a proper shoe store. They were on Third Avenue, which brimmed with Upper East Side expensive choices. *Step on it, Jeeves. Tick-tock!* She had class in an hour, and her seniors weren't very Zen about being made to wait.

"They're ten-dollar drugstore flip-flops," she insisted impatiently. "And I only lost one. So why not give me five dollars of the hundred he slipped you and we'll call it a day?"

James's eyes met Sidra's in the rearview mirror. "I promised him we'd get you proper shoes, miss."

Of course they had to be proper. Sidra could still hear Mr. Import's oh-so-proper accent ringing in her ears. So smooth. "Pretty elaborate pickup technique, don't you think?"

"Or just a good Samaritan, I suppose."

Sidra contemplated James's reply. For a smooth talker, her Prince Charming hadn't offered up a name, or asked for hers. Perhaps this was just one of those weird pay-it-forward things, like covering the toll of the car behind you, or treating the next customer in line at the drive-thru. Manhattan usually didn't see such random acts of senseless kindness. Or, at least, Sidra didn't.

"Here we are, miss."

Sidra balked at the storefront; she recognized the name brand from flipping through those thick fashion magazines her friend Fiona was partial to.

"Um, the hundred dollars he gave you isn't going to buy an Odor-Eater in this store, James."

Her driver reddened as he ushered her through the front door. "That was just my, um . . . tip. Everything else is on the company account."

Sidra felt her ears burn. As if it weren't embarrassing enough to walk into a high-end boutique wearing a paper hospital bootie! "I'm sorry," she mumbled. "I shouldn't have assumed."

Thankfully, the sales girls didn't bat an eye at Sidra's odd choice of footwear and went to fetch her size. "Just the cheapest you've got. Last season," Sidra called after them. They enlisted James, who brought her a sizable stack of boxes. Even the cardboard looked expensive.

"This is ridiculous," she said to no one in particular. Half the styles she nixed just on the prices alone. The other half she longed to play dress-up with, as they were flirty and fun but totally not practical for walking the uneven and broken sidewalks of her East Village neighborhood. James stood by at the ready, as if he had all the time in the world. But Sidra knew time was a-wasting; she had to get back downtown to teach her beginners class at Evolve.

She slid her feet into the most comfortable and decadent pair of flip-flops she had ever encountered. The suede-covered cork footbed practically sighed as it molded around her foot and supported her arch and heel. The straps were genuine black patent leather, not the plastic stuff, and heavily embellished with rhinestones.

"These are perfect. I'll take them."

James looked on approvingly, and for a millisecond, Sidra entertained a fantasy that instead of a suited chauffeur, her Mr. Import was standing there in all his fineness and finery, helping her choose. A pang of regret reverberated through her. She should have at least asked him his name. Not that it mattered, but . . .

A salesgirl discreetly disposed of the dirty paper shoe while the other clerk rang up the purchase. Sidra cringed at the price, knowing her new flip-flops cost roughly eighteen times more than her old pair.

"What's your return policy?" she asked as James supplied Mr. Import's line of credit. She had half a mind to bring the pretty shoes back tomorrow. Although the other half of her brain must've been connected to her feet, which insisted she was never going to take them off.

"Thirty days. Would you like to keep this?" The salesgirl held up Sidra's lone cheap flip-flop.

"Sure, what the heck." Perhaps she'd tack it to her bedroom wall. It could serve as a reminder that Manhattan hadn't run dry of the good guys just yet.

The limo glided down Second Avenue. Sidra made good use of the surround sound stereo and had James rocking rhymes with the Beastie Boys and singing along to seventies Motown by the time they had reached Houston.

"So this is it, I guess."

"It's been a pleasure, miss."

"Please, call me Sidra."

But it was a little too late for introductions, as the limo pulled away from the dusty, littered curb of Rivington Street and the spell was broken.

Back to reality, I guess.

Sidra glanced up as she gave the doorknob of her family's building a vigorous pull. There was the old sign for Sullivan and Son Bicycles, its red and black letters barely legible amidst the curls of peeling paint and splintered swollen wood. Nailed to its bottom frame was the sign Seamus had painstakingly designed and airbrushed for their cousin Mike: a biomechanical steampunk logo for Revolve Records. While the name was fitting for an establishment that still sold physical forms of music, it was really more of an homage to their family's old trade. Although, Sidra thought grimly, Revolve was quickly on its way to becoming a relic itself. Besides Mikey and a few other purists, no one cared about vinyl. Or even CDs anymore, for that matter. Seamus kidded about just airbrushing over the *R* in the sign once the record store flopped. "Evolve or die," he had joked.

Which was how Sidra came to name Evolve, her month-old business.

She really should have a sign made, too. Word of mouth could only travel so far. Still, it secretly pleased her to know her unlabeled yoga studio brought more income into the property during that short time period than her cousin's record sales had in the last quarter.

"Nice shoes." He whistled from behind the counter. "What, did you mug Paris Hilton?"

"All the better to kick you with, Mikey."

Sidra blew her cousin a kiss as she breezed through the deserted record store and into her back sanctuary. Judging from the number of attendance cards out and lockers in use, it looked like she had ten students waiting for her.

"Good afternoon, everyone." She kicked off her overpriced flip-flops. "Let's begin in Child's pose."

Shedding her tunic in favor of the lightweight black tank top underneath, she grabbed her mat and spread it under the light and shadows cast by the lone Moroccan-style brass lamp hanging high in the back space she had claimed as her own.

All of her seniors folded up and rested their torsos on their thighs like dutiful children. *"Balasana."* Sidra breathed the Sanskrit name as everyone, herself included, surrendered to gravity and the state of non-doing required of this pose. As her forehead met her mat, she was grateful for an excuse to clear her mind of the surreal events of the day.

ACKNOWLEDGMENTS

Thank you to all the readers, bloggers, reviewers and librarians who inspired me to spin this heavy metal fairy tale. Your letters and emails, your comments, reviews and word-of-mouth recommendations continue to breathe life into Adrian, Kat and Abbey long after "THE END" was written on Louder Than Love. And your love of these characters brings new dimension to them, beyond my wildest (and deepest) dreams. Through your words, I learn something new about them every day, which fuels me to write more words. Thank you for supporting the book of my heart, and I hope you continue to enjoy the rest of the LOVE & STEEL series. I welcome your feedback and questions, so please feel free to reach out to me at jess@ jesstopper.com - you rock!

ABOUT THE AUTHOR

Jessica Topper has been in love with the beauty of the written word ever since she memorized Maurice Sendak's *Chicken Soup with Rice* at the age of three.

After earning a B.A. in English Literature and her Master's Degree in Library Science, Jessica went on to work as a librarian in New York City before trading in the books for book-keeping. For seventeen years, she worked in the production office of an international touring rock band.

Jessica broke the rock romance mold with her 2013 debut novel LOUDER THAN LOVE. Her follow-up romantic comedy, DICTATORSHIP OF THE DRESS, was named one of Publishers Weekly's Best Books of 2015.

She lives in Western New York with her family - including two cats that love to walk across her keyboard.

Visit her online at jessicatopper.com

ALSO BY JESSICA TOPPER

The "Love & Steel" series:

Louder Than Love

Deeper Than Dreams

Softer Than Steel

More Than Merry

The "Much 'I Do' About Nothing" series:

Dictatorship of the Dress

Courtship of The Cake

Sign up for Jessica's newsletter for exclusive content, news, giveaways and more!

https://tinyletter.com/jesstopper